SKILLS

Published by Lamplight Press, Austin, TX

Cover Design by Rebecca Byrd Arthur
Interior Design by Danielle H. Acee

Library of Congress Cataloguing-in Publication
Denmark, K.
SKILLS / K. Denmark
Subjects: Fiction | American Liteartue | City Life | 20th Century | Motion Pictures | Acting
p. cm.
Library of Congress Control Number: 2023903428
Classification LCC: PS 221 3566 A4554 C68 D2023

Paperback ISBN: 979-8-218-15875-0

SKILLS

k. denmark

last looks: prologue to hunger

Back flip to the end of the 20th century. Word of mouth still existed in full force without the constant heft of devices hurling all into the ether. And the new york city acting community still perused the trades bought at newsstands for audition notices and ads for classes. Classes. Classes guaranteed to constantly improve/create acting skills, voice skills, dance skills, juggling skills until the true skill became making money. For themselves. For the entourage of all that feeds the bank. But now, this time, this year, secret lives could still be kept, secret worlds inhabited without the threat of an internet instant reveal. Résumés easily embedded wild embellishments, small lies elegant and untraceable. Who would know? Or care? The world didn't scavenge for every nugget of truth or revel as universally in the destruction that truth often empowered. And yes, destruction lurks when hunger compels. See me. I am forever locked in a frame of film.

the ads

1. WILL YOU BE READY?
2. FORGET READY FOR YOUR CLOSE-UP.
   WILL YOU BE READY FOR YOUR SEX SCENE?
3. THE GYM? THE ARMY? PRISON?
   NONE OF THEM PREPARE YOU FOR YOUR SEX SCENE.
4. REEL LIFE IS NEVER REALITY WHEN IT COMES TO YOUR SEX SCENE.
5. AMATEUR TAPES ARE JUST THAT.
   WILL YOU BE READY FOR YOUR SEX SCENE?

Calvert ran them in a loop. Sometimes two in an issue. With just his extremely small font phone number at the bottom after an anticipatory lull of blank newspaper space. He knew the readership of BroadLights Weekly. It was the young, the students, the stage mothers, the wannabees, the ignorant, the amateur retirees. All hungry to be in that womb-like heat of the inner circle, the known faces, the ones who never again had to ache over price tags.

Calvert glanced over at Valerie. She was midway through The Wall Street Journal. And that one, millions. Millions, every year now. And still makes us use the hand soap until the last wee flake. She outright adores that antique contraption to put all the bits and pieces in a stingy metal cage and shake it up and whoopee! new invention. Soap. First thing I do when you are gone. When the money is mine. Fresh bar of soap every week. No. Every goddamned day.

Valerie gave Calvert a small smile. It didn't cover up the wafting stench of her almost silent pop of gas. She always smiled at gas. Did she think it was cute?

He went back to the ads. A necessary business expense. The hungry would think it was cool, hip, groovy, whatever the word of the day was. The tiny font was the narrow door of the unmarked club beckoning them in. Those who had made it no longer needed to buy that glorified advice column masquerading as journalism. The needy are my audience. The needy shall seek me out. They always do.

He had the power of want. They want something, anything that will give them an imagined edge over the other five million hopelessly hopeful. The power of want. And the fools will scarcely suspect I have nothing.

He breathed in deeply to calm his body, close his brain. How on earth did I get here? I feel infused with bitters three-quarters of the day.

He did love Valerie. I do love Valerie. The weight. It is not about the weight. I actually prefer the heft of her now. Her warmth is delicious. My personal pot-bellied stove come winter in this drafty loft. Boredom? It has been so, yes. She works. I audition. I do not audition. I never audition. I teach. She works. I teach something totally new. And I finally have a good time.

See Dick run. See Jane fall. See Dick take her from behind.

But the class was still pocket change. Just enough to augment his blue I'm so blue Monday allowance check from darling Valerie.

Valerie. Come over here, my darling. My shoulders are tight.
Hang onto the grab bar. I'm reading.
Valerie, are you being rebellious?

Not even a look. Not that I need you. Calvert moved the nail of his index finger slowly up his penis still flaccid beneath his charcoal worsted pants. He shut his eyes and left the room. Mister Blessing has left the house, folks. Calvert smiled for their sadness. His fans.

george gowerlich

Yeah, so I'm not good looking. So what? I got what the girls want. If the girls knew. I got a big schlong. I got a great big schlong. A big cock. A giant, monster dick. If the girls knew. If the girls just knew.

I been thinking about the nature tv. Gotta love the nature tv. The bears. The lions running. Sometimes they even got humping nature tv. I especially like the one when they show a flower grow. Up up over time. How do they do that? Is it slow motion? Maybe. Or they keep the camera there for weeks and weeks and someone must have to come back and dust off the camera and put in more film or something. It interests me how my schlong grows. Can't really see it. It just happens. I'd like to see it. Just like the nature tv. I'd like to watch it grow in slow motion. If a girl could watch it too.

Maybe this semester will be different. And we'll watch it together. Yeah, that's how it'll be.

almost asleep but not

Pammy settled into bed. A true single bed not even a twin. A true single bed with barely room to sling a leg or turn or twist. With sheets of beige and a warm cocoa blanket to wrap up tight in.

It was just lying there in the reception area at work. Someone must have left it when they got called into an appointment. If I had seen who it was, I would have made sure they got it back. But I didn't see. And now it's mine. I didn't steal it. It was just lying there on the table. BroadLights. It felt like glamour. It felt like the key.

She devoured it on the subway and Cal's ad devoured her. It leaped into her fantasies and followed her into her brown single bed.

She thought taking the class would be a good way to lose her virginity. Surely someone will sleep with me there. Surely only really sexy people would take such a class. Sex-filled people. I'm sex-filled. No. I am sex unfilled. Fill me. Fill me. Where do I sign up?

When she masturbated, she had huge boobs and endless legs. The first time she had an orgasm was a totally unplanned surprise. She was reading a book. What book was I reading? I can't remember. I was just squeezing my thighs together for no particular reason. Squeezing and squeezing and then the squeezing became more important than the reading. And then boom! I got this weird feeling and it was kind of nice.

That was two years ago. After a while, it seemed like a lot of work to squish her thighs. She knew where the feeling came from. She touched it. It was where she got her period and the smells that scared her. Made her think she was dying. She was still too terrified to take a mirror and see what it looked like. Someday, but not now. Now I'm going to get the good feeling 'cause I have a good feeling about this class. I mean if I take it, that is.

She touched herself. But touching alone would no longer do the sexual trick, wake the magic, warm the juices still so surprising to her. Now she needed to mentally transform herself to make it happen. She was a dirty girl, a slut. With the boobs, the legs, the underwear like the models wore. Afterwards, she religiously cleaned herself with a hot washcloth and soap. Just in case she smelled.

Sometimes I do. That's true. When I have my period and all those pads. She changed pads on the hour and wrapped them in so much toilet paper they resembled snowballs crowding the little pink garbage pail in the bathroom she shared with Mother.

But if someone wanted to sleep with me, what would I do? Would I have time to excuse myself to go into the bathroom and wash myself? Would he say I smelled? Would he smell? What kind of smell do boys have anyhow?

Oh, God. When I think about taking this class, I'm breathing wind. I'm jumping off a bridge. I have to jump. I just have to.

my name is really seamus, really cohen

Seamus lived in a 200 square foot apartment in a much divided townhouse on 24th Street off Ninth. He had a light gray couch futon on an oak frame which, as a point of discipline, he made up every morning. Sheets, pillow and blanket were neatly folded and hidden behind a paper screen. Last week, he bought a bright red throw pillow to add focus. He had painted each wall of the tiny studio 20x10 a different color. A deep teal. Red. A pale amber. Charcoal. He would eat facing just one wall as if it were the color of an entire room. Seamus had created his four room apartment.

The once elegant townhouse had been butchered into efficiency apartments. He spent hours imagining the past of his room. A beribboned pale woman in a long purple dress dances into his head. He spots the imprint of the track for French doors that once separated the parlor. Etched glass? Flowers dripping? He knew the parquet on his floor was the original. But the gaps and the holes? No, it was once a perfect floor, for perfect feet in shoes of glove leather made by hand. Shoes for the purple enchantress.

Seamus sold that essay to one of those giveaway society glossies the Park Avenue folk find stacked on a fine piece of lobby furniture. The type of magazine where they never read the articles but only look for themselves in the pictures taken at various charity events and who's wearing what and who's sitting with whom. Seamus knew he would never be a whom. On the other hand, that was not entirely out of the picture. He could become a "walker," the unmarried, usually gay, man on a society arm. But a walker had to have good patter, good connections, good dancing chops. Okay, strike that fantasy.
I am an observer not a charmer.

On moving in, he put up a mezuzah on his door, careful to position it correctly, facing inward. He had to use his favorite reference book, "To Be A Jew," to recite the correct prayer, the correct brokhe. Why am I so unknowledgeable about my own religion? But there must be other dolts about or why would this book even exist? After he put up the mezuzah, he noticed the imprint of a long-gone mezuzah on a neighbor's door. Then he saw another ghost of a mezuzah by a candy store down the block. That essay he sold to the English edition of The Forward, "The Ghost Mezuzahs Of Chelsea."

So, are you a famous writer yet?
I piece it together, Dad.

Yeah, I piece it together, Pulitzer Dad. He never told him he came to nyc to act. He never told him he wasn't going into the family business, so to speak. Journalists all, even going back to the Old Country, to Poland. Seamus wanted someone else's words to guide him. He wanted someone else's words to pop from his mouth, transform him into a different man. Is that what they all do? Those members of the acting tribe? A ritual verbal initiation the first time words incite another you?

His Mom still mailed him a secret $150 dollars a month. It made a big difference. Maybe she knows.

super glue

The counselor had urged her over and over. So finally she went to one of those stupid survivor groups. Oh, you think you were abused? Why did she go in the first place? I was talked into it. I don't take orders no more. I don't. Oh, you think you were abused? Your uncle? Your father? Your sixteen brothers? Was it abuse 'cause you knew it was abuse? Something felt hinky? Made your skin withdraw? What if you thought it was normal? Something all little girls did from as long as they could remember.

Last night, on tv, that ad for diapers. And the mom is doing the belly dance with the baby. Kissy kissy on her tummy and the baby just giggles away. Just giggles away.

I have to get rid of this. I have to get this poison out of me. Like parasite larva deposited and growing and clawing and eating me from inside. Out out damn spot. That's what the group home lady would always say. Out.

Take your story and pretend it's a story about somebody else, the counselor say. Who would have this story? In the movies even, this story is too – None of these group girls could make it up. And look, they's all married and some with kids and they made a life. Why keep complaining? Look at me. Look at me.

Yeah, I got a job. At a big office. And everything on the outside is clean. But I shut my eyes and hell be waking.

at the charcoburger

Gradually, they all piled into the bar from The SGK Studio. Most paid per session. Some had rich parents forking up for the whole year. Usually, those ones didn't hang at The Charcoburger. But the crowd at Charcoburger nursed the student discount beer and shared fries. They argued if ketchup was a sauce in the truest sense of Julia Child. Bragged and lied about auditions. Eyed each other to see if they could steal a look, the wave of hair, the right amount of eye shadow or army fatigue.

No. The OneLegUp is the place to go. For ten bucks you can meet an agent. You do a monologue. Hand them your shots. Have a little chit chat all under four minutes. And that ten buck investment got me a call for a meeting.

How'd it go?
It's for next week.

Next week never comes. Next week hopes no one will remember the conversation for this week and ask how next week went. So many next weeks they all have, they know not to remember for fear someone will remember theirs.

His hair had the strange flat yellow color of a legal pad. Anton Grybowski was a big guy, eager and earnest. I have no audition. I have no agent meeting. I have no nothing to say. Oh, yes. Wait, wait I want to be part of this group. My fellow actors. My Americans. His voice was too big for the room and, like a child, he didn't know how loud he was or how to modulate it.

I'm taking now a class for sex.

The table quiets and focuses on him.

Is that the one that always advertises in BroadLights?
How often do you go?
Do you have to be naked?

It was Chester who asked that last question. Chester Rootberry fresh up north from Orlando, land o' Disney. Fantasy in his blood, dripped in through Mickey Mouse ears, mother's milk cotton candy dna.

Do you have to be naked?

Chester thought about his skinny arms and flat little boy chest. He thought about all the push and pressure to buff up, take to the gym, worship weights. For what? The not-so-silent implication that that would get him roles as a bouncer, a bodyguard, a criminal? Yeah, right. The modern day equivalent of the 1930's mammy or butler roles. Yeah, like Stepin Fetchet but now it's Stepin Slug'emout. Well, that's not going to be me. Not me. If you offer me a protein drink, I will shoot you in my head.

Do you have real sex in the class?

Anton dodged giving answers as best he could. Maybe this I should not have said.

They make us keep secret the inside of the class. We talk hockey now, yes? Gretzky's hat trick last night. Some wow.

I must keep more careful what I say. But it was nice to be the center of all eyes. My Americans. But if they ask me more? If they ask me again? Maybe I find the ad and I take the class for true. But how much money? Always the money.

Chester Rootberry had no interest in hockey. He did have an interest in becoming Chet, his actor name. Chet Root. It sounded fast and hard. Suave and James Bond. Even Aunt Myrt thought it was a good choice. Chet would know all the moves in his tuxedo and black bow tie and cummerbund and patent leather shoes. Chet would take the class.

dear

Dear Teenie –

You know I told you I was taking this class – a scene study class at the SGK Studio? Maybe I didn't. No, I didn't. Well, it's a school where all the big names started out. All your favorites in the black and white films. That's me in a black and white film. Ha Ha. Mostly white and me – the black. Get it? Anyhow the other night this guy was talking about another class he thought was really something. Something to take me up another level as an actor and I think I may drop this one and take that one. It's something that will make me stretch as an actor and when you're an actor that's what you want to do. Stretching is like taking yourself as far as you can go. Or like somebody you always think is a comedian doing Shakespeare. Serious stuff. Like testing yourself, you know. Playing a part so different from you that you got to lose yourself to make it work. To the outer limits Teenie! That will be your shy little brother.

I miss you. – Chet (my new name!!!)

off the bus

The brown hair she left behind. The moment she got to Port Authority, she asked a girl about her age, a blond of course, where was a drug store to get some hair dye. Lucky for her, imagine that, it was another actress on her way to a dinner theatre – that's theatre with an r-e — in Pennsylvania. Another actress. I'm an actress. From the moment I got on the bus. I'm officially an actress just like this girl. And they talked a lot. The helper actress and the newbie. I'm in a dream. Me. This is fiction. But no.

Not a soul helped me when I came to the city from Erie, so I'm going to help you. In fact, some people in this very terminal tried to trick me. But that's not me. I'm giving you the straight scoop for all the best stuff, hair and everything.
Gee, thanks.

And she said the only place to go was Ray's Beauty Supplies on 8th Avenue and 44th. Wow, that girl really knew. Ray's was just magic. It was theatre beauty. Show business beauty stuff you could tell right away. Even plastic aprons so you don't spill dye on yourself. And on top of all that, that Port Authority actress,

Janine, she even gave her a telephone number of some friends looking for a roommate. This was just too good. This was a sign.

Blond hair, done. Roof over the head, done. And already newly blond new york Wissa Antoine is working as a waitress at a bar on the upper east side. Dolan's, right on First Avenue. Her roommates told her working in that neighborhood would mean good tips. "The upper east side is very shi-shi-wah-wah," they chimed. They were vocalists. All three of them. Wissa believed them. Until she looked around and saw the dividing line. West of Lexington was money. The far east? Loads of tenements still with bathroom down the hall.

Just three weeks into the job at Dolan's, she abandoned those ignorant roommates on east 5th street. What do they know? For the same money as my share, this waiter told me about an apartment right nearby on East 73rd Street by the river for only $375 a month. Right next to the Sanitation Garage. My own place. A one bedroom. With a sort of living room and a squeezed in kitchen and a really tiny bathroom. Three hundred twenty-five square feet. I saw it. I rented it.

The first thing Wissa did when she got her own place, besides buying a futon, would never be anything she thought. Not ever have thought. Not dishes. Not towels or even hangers. (The vocalists would not let her take even one. And dry cleaner's wire at that.) The first thing Wissa did was to buy a corn husk broom and a dust pan. Something about the deep blue of the wooden handle and the sound of the bristles dancing across the floor. I am a pioneer in my world. Mine.

What is that closet in the middle of the hallway? Oh. It's the bathroom for the two other apartments down the hall. The rent controlled apartments. One of them is where the twin sisters live.

Oh, my sweet little dear. Welcome to the building.
Welcome to the building.
We've lived here our whole lives. Just forever.
Ever and ever.
That horrible new landlord set fires to the building to get the rent controlled tenants to leave.
To leave in the middle of the night. Just so he could build bathrooms.
Mr. Kovac lived in your apartment. He's dead now.
Dead? Like from the fires? The landlord did that?
No, no, no sweetness. From an appendicitis before the fires.
Before.

The twins dressed alike. They dressed alike and wore white gloves. Wissa wondered if they were virgins. They giggled a lot. She imagined them getting undressed very modestly. Maybe even they never looked at their own crotches. Or touched themselves. Wissa coveted their wardrobe stopped in time. Prim shirtwaist dresses from the fifties. Cinch belts and pert little chiffon scarves tied around the ropey tendons of their aging necks. Do they have matching poodle skirts in their closets? Can I have your poodle skirt, please?

And now it's one year later. One year chasing auditions and hoarding tips. Look at me. I can line up four dishes on my left arm and hold one on my right. I can remember who wants what and how they want it. I can remember their faces when they come through the door. But that guy at The Limelight last week? I think he had curly hair. His penis was hard and pink. They are all body parts. I'm a body part. The plates cover the scars on my arms so no one will ask. How dare you ask? What makes everyone assume it's their right to know? I got attacked by a lion in the circus. Are you going to say I'm lying? I leave you all behind in Mashpee, the hip place of the not so hip. Where my only worth was between my thighs. Or so I thought. No. I knew. Goodbye to you. Not so good but bye. I am a hot chick in New York City. A woman. I have my own place and a job and a headshot and a tomorrow in capital letters. Wissa looked in the mirror. Oh damn. I'm getting a zit. She remembered the headline: WILL YOU BE READY? Hmmm, not unless I can camouflage this thing on my nose.

maura felix

The receptionist behind the desk looked at her expectantly. Maura surreptitiously dialed her landline from her cell phone. Her answering machine picked up. She waited politely for the beep.

I can't believe I'm getting your answering machine. Where are you? They won't let me leave without someone picking me up. Call me.

Maura hung up. The receptionist, as planned, had overheard.

We really can't let you leave after a colonoscopy without an escort.
I'm not woozy. I feel fine. I live two blocks away. I have no idea where my friend Sally is.

The receptionist looked up at the wall clock. 5:45. Maura had intentionally made the appointment for late afternoon. She timed it for this outcome. She didn't have a friend named Sally. In fact, as the years meandered by, she had fewer and fewer friends. And I'm not going to ask them to come pick me up after my welcome to old age test. I'm fine. I don't need help.

She refused to ask anyone for help. She looked around at the two couples getting ready to leave from the waiting room. Old. Young. Lumpy. Attractive. A cover for every pot. Where's my cover? Oh, Gus. I miss you.

All right. You can go. But promise me, Ms. Felix, you'll take a cab. For two blocks? Okay, I promise.

Like shit I will. Did I say that? Dad would say I'm cussing like a salty sailor. I refuse to drown in a sea of widows, keeping to my "own kind." She remembered her father's disdain for widows. Hated hosting the wives of friends long gone. Her mother complained. Wouldn't you want someone to socialize with me if you were gone? But I'm not gone. I'm not going nowhere. That was always his reply.

But go he did. They all do. Since Gus died, Maura had been sleeping around. Why am I so attractive to married men? But the strings don't pull. Sometimes she worries, in particular, she will be introduced by some weird chance to that wife who owns a gallery on Madison. Oh you're Herbie's wife. I used to know him, fuck him, blow him. Fervently. Used to, as in three days ago. And if I did meet her, would she even care? He loves her. He's proud to be seen with her. He doesn't drop his hand like touching a hot iron when he realizes it's around her shoulder and God forbid he's in public. I'm nothing to her. To him. Sometimes I wonder how much I was even to Gus.

I've got to shake it up. Otherwise I'm going down down down. I'll take a class. That's what I'll do. Something totally out of my realm. I'll shake it up. Poker? Esperanto? Juggling? Right. Me juggling bowling pins. I can see it now.

There was still snow on Broadway and 92nd Street. Maura walked over to the newsstand. Not quite sure what she was looking for. Where do they advertise classes? Her eyes danced over all the magazines, the newspapers.

I'll take this one.
One fifty, lady.

Two blocks. No way I'm taking a cab. Like a child she kicked at a snow pile and stomped north. At the light, she flipped open BroadLights. There it was. Calvert's ad.

loft d

The elevator had an out of order sign on it so Pammy began climbing the stairs to Loft D. Big wide wooden stairs. Maybe five feet wide. Why so wide? Pammy wondered. So they could carry up big heavy iron machines. Cast iron. Big men hunched over with straps tight around the machines on their backs. She imagined them with leather shoes and newsboy caps and shirt-sleeves rolled up on thick, thick muscles. Sweating. No one ever wore t-shirts then or had a bare head or...... or maybe the steps are wide so the workers could flee? Run in their long skirts and dresses from the fire raging. Sparks igniting in the dust of generations of fabric. Run! Run! Run ladies run. Because they were ladies not girls. Or do I have it wrong? They were girls because they worked. They were ladies if their hands were like pillows. No hands like that on these stairs. Hands like that. Hands like that in my grandmother's lap. Holding me.

Pammy was thin but she didn't exercise and each flight of stairs was a mountain. Then the door marked "D" filled her eyes. But there's no bell. There's no bell and I'll have to knock and no one will hear me. No one ever hears me.

She knocked. She knocked again. And louder.
Footsteps. And the door creaked open. Cal boomed in his actor voice:

Ah, our last, much awaited attendee. Do not just stand there. Find a seat. And a tissue. You're sweating.

the surround

It was a large room. Large by apartment standards not loft standards. Several severely worn Persian rugs clung to the planks of the wooden floor. Exposed pipes explored the vertical. Exposed bricks held bits of ancient plaster on the walls. Books. Books shelved and piled. Books with slips of newspaper crammed in to mark a spot.

Mismatched folding chairs held the eight student bottoms. Cal stood now but waiting for him was a king chair. Oh definitely, a king chair. Carved mahogany with great arms rounded into dragon's heads. Clawed feet. Anton searched his English vocabulary. Not a king chair. A throne.

Who am I ? Besides an intriguing ad in your beloved BroadLights Weekly, I am, of course, an actor. Past and present. G. Calvert Blessing for your listening enjoyment. My students call me Cal. My friends call me as often as possible. My lovers call out for mercy.

He waited a beat for applause but settled for their tentative giggles.

The well-practiced monologue continued. As he reeled off each non-truth, fattened truth, he clarified it in his head.

I was considered to be one of my generation's up and coming Shakespearean actors.
(In the Witchie Witchie Iowa Community Theater.)
Acclaimed in Dresden.
(Ah claimed to be in Dresden, but no sir, ah was not.)
He proceeded down his résumé. Oh god. That girl is taking notes.

Pammy stopped writing at his silence and looked up expectantly. His eyes are right on me. He likes me.

Cal clutched some headshots in his hand. He dropped them into an old metal milk crate. He held onto the students' sign-in sheet.

Not all of you have headshots, I see. Perhaps you will have invested in them by the end of the course. Nevertheless, we will deal with the headshots and résumés later. Perhaps never. That sort of information is public domain. This, as well you know, is not your traditional class. But we will break with the non-traditional and trade names. Full names. I do not want to know your background. Or your dreams. Even your so-called training. Just the facts, ma'am. (Oh my, no one got that reference. Perhaps their grandmothers remember Joe Friday.) Names. Names only. Even though it is always more fun to fuck a stranger.

Pammy panicked. Did he say that? I thought this was pretend. At least, in the class, that is. I never even thought of that. I just thought I might meet someone to date, to—

Calvert pointed at Chet to start. Can't say Chester now. Not here. Time to use my actor name. Here goes.

Chet Root.
Wissa Antoine.
Maura Felix.
Anton Grybowski.

George looked around the class. If I was ever to have a sex scene it would be here. For certain. Not even a comedy would cast my hairy butt. Assuming I could act. Which I can't. And all those girls are all eyes for Cal. Just like last semester. Can I lower my voice? Do I have an actor voice too? He lowered his voice several octaves from his natural comfort zone.

George Gowerlich.
Do you have a cold, George? Because I believe in kindness. You do not come to class to spread germs.
No, I'm fine.

Bibi. Bibi De Los Santos.
Seamus Cohen.

Calvert glanced again at the list.
And you must be — Pammy. Little miss Pammy Kemple. That is exactly your name?
Pammy nodded.
Ghastly. At least you could go for Pamela. This isn't 1965, you know.
The seven other classmates laughed on cue. Not sure why.

Pammy is the name on my birth certificate.
My dear, true actors do not even remember having a birth certificate.

the spiel

I will be a hard teacher. In every sense but that. I will be honest and break your spine if I have to.
All this Calvert says with his pale gray, red-veined eyes boring into Pammy's.
I will care for you.
And Pammy is in love.

No talking. No answers from the peanut gallery. This is a rhetorical question: What do you truly know about how sex scenes are filmed?
Anton: I hear—
Do you not know what rhetorical means?
Anton shakes his head "no."
In this room it means a question for me to ask and for me to answer.
Yes, sir.

Cal took a second look at this big, long-haired brute. I could enjoy someone who calls me "sir."

Now, how exactly do they film a sex scene? Certainly not with two people on a bed. Three if you are gifted. No. You need a director. The waters will part for him or her. You need a camera and someone to operate it. A director of photography to make the lighting superb, the angles enticing and electricians to carry out that plan. Grips are required to set flags to ensure that that lighting is even more subtle or to lay track for the dolly under the camera to creep around your bed. The dolly cannot move itself, so you also need a grip to push it. A pimple has erupted on your sweet behind. The make-up artists must erase it and the sweat of desire – a.k.a. glycerin – must be sprayed on you as well. Think there is no wardrobe involved? Think again. The wardrobe department will do its best to "dress" you to look naked even though you are not. They have all sorts of delicious tricks from pasties to cock socks. And if your bush or chest hair just is not up to par, make-up comes back at you again, dedicated to augmenting the hair-challenged. A merkin appears. Look that up in the dictionary, children. That sheet, so artfully draped over your thigh? Thank the set dresser for that. The sighs and moans recorded for posterity? A boom operator will be over you with a microphone on a pole while the sound mixer records. They may even cleverly hide a microphone on the headboard — whatever they deem most efficient. And on top of that massive crowd is a script supervisor to make sure everyone is doing their job so all will match for the esteemed editor. And what do I mean by that? For example, that drop of sweat must always, always be just one half inch to the right of that mole on your cheek. And that pillow you knocked off the bed in the play of passion must find its way back to the precise square one before every take.

Oh yes, they may, as they say "clear the set" for actual filming, but even a minimal crew could be at least three other souls. And, of course, between takes, three-quarters of the crew will come scurrying back to adjust, re-set and discuss how to make it better. You? You great Shakespearean actor are no more than a meat puppet to some of them. Oh naturally you will be treated with respect but you are merely part of the whole and they are just as important as you in making it all work. This you must remember.

If you want to go the diva route, that is your call regardless of gender. But no one will forget. Even the third grip. Your name will be passed around like an hors d'oeuvre. I remember when I worked with him. What an asshole.

Cal thought back to that time when he was battling constipation in a stall in the men's room at EUE Stages and overheard two grips talking about him. Chilling. A commercial for a brokerage company. I was an excellent spokesman. The director was hot for my voice. But those grips. They remembered me from "Teacher's Holiday." Damn you Valerie. All your fault. You had me in circles with love. I couldn't function. You filled my head. I needed you everywhere. Hell, I was young. So young, I insisted that your photograph be near me at all times. I railed that your addictive face be allowed to rest carefully on the floor just outside of the frame line. That demand preceded every shot. Oh, how very much I needed you to calm me during my first lead role.

And my last.

"This guy, Blessing, " one grip laughed. "He was the one from that no-budget teacher film we did down in North Carolina. Remember? Around '69? '70?"
"The one with the shrine to his girlfriend?"

"Yep. Total ass. Total."

Cal surveyed the class.

It is not just or even just. It is not just having sex. It is your character. As any good actor knows, you must breathe your character, eat as he eats, walk as he would, sigh as he would. When you are developing your character's back story, you develop their complete being. You give them a fuller life than the writer could ever imagine.

I doubt that's the writer's opinion, Maura mused. But, like most thoughts, she kept that to herself.

Cal continued: You create their inner life. For instance, a favorite color.

He notices Pammy is off in the clouds.

You. Stop daydreaming. What is your particular favorite color?
Mine? Uh, brown.
Brown? Brown? Could you be any more revealing, my darling? You are truly a naked woman when you declare your favorite color to be brown. Perhaps more than naked. Transparent. Not much going on there, I suspect.

Every particle of Pammy shrinks. Cal continues his ramble.

But I digress. Remember that on a set, you are not alone. You are never alone. Tonight when you sleep with your lover, your mate or masturbate with your faithful hand, I want you to think about all the other people who could be in the room with you. I want you to think about doing it, acting it, over and over until your wrist hurts and your knees feel arthritic. Take after take after take. What could be achieved in less than ten minutes for some of us—

Why is he looking at me? He is looking at me. George starts twirling the curly hair of his beard to calm himself.

What could take less than ten minutes for some of us, can take over five hours on a set. Reel – r-e-e-l — time is not r-e-a-l time. But you still have to relate to your fellow actor. You are in this together. That is why we are here. Are you ready? Are you up for it?

He waited for a response. All eight just stared at him.

What is the matter with all of you? Can you not speak?

Wissa: Oh, can we talk now?
Who denied you permission?

adios étudiants

Cal pulled out his pocket watch and examined it slowly so they could all fully appreciate the object and the act.

We will gather again next week. You have your assignment but I will add one more item. Go see or rent a film with some racy scenes. No porn. That does not count. Simulation is the act we are studying. Instead of falling into the story as an audience member, I want you to view it from without. Where is your imagination filling in the blanks? What blanks did they leave you to fill in? Is that really your favorite celebrity or a body double?

Where is my body double to replace this body with its old man love handles? Where did they come from? And that vague thin patch of hair at the back of my head? Cannot even bear to pick up Valerie's gilded hand mirror anymore. Shut my eyes and it is not there. Shut my eyes and these young girls will eye me as a probability. No. Open my eyes and what do I see? They see me not. They lust no more.

That will be all, my new students. You may leave your payment for this week on my desk. Please note, though, and this is very important, that for the remaining classes in the semester I will accept only money orders. Money orders on my desk at the beginning of class. This first class is the exception. No rubber checks. No crumpled cash. The very act of arriving with a money order proves to me that you are truly committed. You have spent the money before you even cross my threshold. No emptying of pockets. No pleading or begging. As I said, money up front, my dears, in the great and wise tradition of whoredom. As I might well be. As might we all.

Everyone felt the verbal wink. Cal most of all. Wissa raises her hand.

But you have to pay an extra fee for a money order.
Yes, you do. Welcome to the business world. Nothing is as it is. There are always hidden, extra fees. It gives the appearance of legitimacy.

As I do, Cal affirms in his glorified brain. Maura absorbs his comment on legitimacy. Did he just say what I thought he said?

Have an enjoyable moment or two with your homework assignments. Toodle loo until next week.

Each one filed by on the way to the door and down the stairs. Wissa paused.

I got an audition tomorrow. For a commercial.
Excellent.
I'm a young mom.
I can see that. Point of advice, Willa –

Wissa. Short for Elizabeth.
Just adorable. Point of advice. Do not wear that low-cut shirt. Unless you plan to breast feed on camera.
Oh. Yeah, sure. Thank you. Bye.

I am such a god. Swallow every word, little ones. All right, I believe a nice long bath is in order after opening night. Calvert turned and was face to face with Anton. He had thought Wissa was last to go. He hadn't heard Anton at all. What was this brute about? Was he hulking beneath one of those spindly ancient wooden fold-up chairs?

Yes?
I think this class will be my improvement. But I see it is that I have some difficulty to pay every week.
Were you aware of that before you arrived here today?
Yes, sir.

Oh, that "sir" gets me every time. And look at him. He is just so damn – big.

Perhaps we can work something out, Anton.
Thank you, sir.

Cal absorbed Anton's body as he left the loft.

Anton trudged down the stairs. How bad this is? Not very bad. I do this now. I do this before and before. I shut the eyes and his old man cock is nothing. A thing. I remove him from the thing and he is nothing. And I win. I get the class. I get the jacket. I get the room I sleep in. I am Anton Grybowski a winner.

after

Gradually they all made it to the street. Some head this way. Some uptown. Some subway. Some foot.

George approaches Pammy.

Brown is the color of the earth. It's warm and it surrounds you.

Pammy's head was full of Calvert. He loves me he hates me he loves me. It always happens for her in an instant. That's how it was. Her eyes didn't even focus on George when she responded.

I have to go home.

Bibi overhears. A small chorus plays in her head. "Brown, brown in the toilet down." Which bright parent sang me that inspirational song? Or maybe it was a mister? Now why would a mister sing me that?

Seamus caught up with Bibi. Something about her. A remoteness topped by that incredible hair. Her hair was like a giant feathery crazy black cloud. A person could hide in that hair. I could hide in that hair. I could write a poem to her hair, words dancing off every strand.

What'd you think?
I don't know. I'm not sure this is for me.
But you want to be an actress.
I'm a paralegal.
Well, we're all something for the rent. I'm a journalist, kind of. But we're really actors, right?

Why does he seem so much younger than me? Redheads is always young but this one. He could be older than me for all I know.

Everybody acts.
Seamus persisted: But you know. You know what I mean. I'm taking the bus. See you next week?

She started to walk away. He stopped her.

That was a question. About seeing you next week.
I know. I'm just not knowing the answer.
Well, if you think of one, here's my card.
You got a fucking card?

Bibi shot down the street. Seamus watched her speed walk into the dark. Well, that went well. Loneliness has an odor. At least I tried. He tucked the unwanted card back into his pocket.

Seamus waited at the bus stop. Must've just missed one. No one's here. A man approached from farther down the street.

Like his look. Tall. All legs. He's got a nice stride and I do love a beard. When he gets close, should I smile? No, it's cooler just to stare. If he knows, he'll know. I would know.

So close now. I can see his face. Very nice. Apples and spice. Even in the shadows, looks good. The man paused and reached up and picked his nose. He wiped his finger on the nearest street tree and continued walking towards the bus stop. He stared hard at Seamus. Gay-dar ahoy. Oh, please, you uncouth bastard, do not take the bus. Seamus looked away. Saved.

Thank you, G-d. Thank you, G-d for saving me from being the fool. My brokhe for the day. My after brokhe. Yes.

the girl who i am

By the time she was twelve, the tutu was very short and raggedy. The Professor arrives and she shuts her eyes. When he's finished, he say to me: Dulce. (All the misters call me Dulce. Mami told them to. She told me never tell the misters your name for true. Your name be Dulce when you wear the tutu and we got misters. So I be Dulce to the Professor 'cause he's a mister but not like the others. I think he's my last mister.)

The Professor say, Dulce, someday I hope you feel this.
Feel what, Professor?
A man will do what I do that you love and it will all be different.
Do you know why I still come to visit?
You the last, Professor.
I visit to see that you are safe.

Then he did the big no-no. The forbidden. He kiss my lips. They's only allowed to kiss down there. Vacuum me up, no fingers, no inside or back side. But the Professor, that day, he kiss my lips but I never tell.

That night I hear Papi Fannon and Mami talk.

He Irish say, "Old enough she is. Small boned, so they might still think she's a wee one. If she wasn't having titties in bloom, I think we could get a 'thou but with those damn titties, only eight."
Mami say, "But she's still my baby."
"Baby got titties. Fannon needs the rent money."

December ten, my birthday, he bring home a rubber dildo. I don't ever forget that day. I never see such a scary thing. It hurt to look at it.

"Homework," Papi Fannon say.
Mami: "That's too big, Fannon. She's still a baby. A baby."
"Not mine. You teach her, bitch. Teach her to take it every which way and take it nice."

He goes slamming out the door and probably hang with his boys like always. Mami, she hundred times brushed my hair and put that ugly rubber cock in the drawer. But I knew what it was. I seen it hanging off the misters. I seen it standing up and standing down. I seen my Mami spit on it and swallow it and make scary gaggy noises on it. And the misters smiling and ohhing and Mami with a funny pretend smile that made me scared she was a pretend Mami and not mine at all.

We do this tomorrow, Bibi. I know you don't understand but I love him. I do anything for him. So you gotta too. You gotta, Bibi. You want your cake now? I got candles.
I give her a big kiss and hug.
No cake. No candles, Mami.
She hug me tighter than I ever remember.

I run away that night. That night I be twelve years old. I never see Mami or Papi Fannon again. Bet they still there. I could keep going on this train straight up to 3589 Broadway and there they be.

She got a chill and looked at the other women on the platform. Bet you played with dolls.

pammy and

Pammy took care of her mother. It just happened that way. Or maybe it was planned to happen that way. There was a ten year gap between her and Connie and Vickie and Steffie and they must have had a powwow some high school day, some St. Agnes of the Bleeding Eyes high school day to figure their advantage. They took one look at Pammy in her crib and booked imaginary tickets up up and away. And Mother sings to me you'll never leave me, my little girl, my gift from God. And Daddy sticks around just long enough for me to remember him thinner and thinner from the hungry cancer until I compared my little girl leg to his and they were both the same.

A good girl figures it out. A good girl figures out she's not really pretty. Not even her Mother bothered to lie. You don't need to try on my make-up. Why bother? Well, if I go on the stage, I'll need to know how to do my make-up. On stage? And Mother's emphysema kicked in with the laughter and choked her and phlegmed her all the way to the bathroom.

Junior year in high school, she read "The Glass Menagerie." If they're writing about girls like Laura, then they're writing about girls like me. Then there are parts that will be easy for me to act in. I can be an actress. I can open my mouth and words will come out. Words that I don't have to think about because they will be the right words. Words a really smart author wrote. A playwright. As long as I can remember them they will be the right words. People will want to get to know me. And laugh with me. Laugh.

But years sped forward unscripted. Pammy's dreams began to smell of dust. One day she came home from work and found Mother scrubbing her face with Brillo. Her arms were all herky jerky and fast. She turned and stared straight through Pammy to the furniture unchanged for generations. The books unread. The good china for no good times. And then, like that, she was Mother again. Red bloodied face and all.

Your sister Connie called today. She's moving to Sarasota. Joining Vickie and that husband of hers. Can't take the winter anymore. Not her knees. Not her back.

Not us, Pammy thought with an empty inhale.

polymath to me; jack to you

I was quite good at the clarinet and was urged to pursue being a musician. But that life. I would have to practice every day. And art. I could do that. Even Valerie's parents found some promise there. Well, admittedly they were on a hunt for crumbs. But to be a painter, one is expected to paint all the time. Be driven. I would prefer a patron. Commissions. Checks in the mail. Money. Perhaps a concubine in lieu.

Even acting. I never went to school. And all this brouhaha about classes. I know what to do. I have always known what to do. Give me a job and I will do it. I was born with a voice and excellent muscles in my brow.

I took the Mensa test. Not everyone knows that. I prefer not to boast. Of course I was accepted. My intelligence is a treasure.

Like many a wunderkind, Calvert's discipline and desire were lacking and his social skills questionable at best. More talent than ambition, his own father had cursed. Cal's life tumbled into a ping pong of procrastination, day dreams and masturbation. Here I am, once again, masturbating. It is very important to me. It is an essential part of my day.

If it is not a day interrupted by Valerie or students, it is a day of peace. I lie in bed or on the couch and exercise my hand. Fame is for fools. But when Valerie drags me to a gallery and I see what passes for art, I always know I could do better.

I could do better in every area. I could top them all. You name them, they are beneath me. I just do not have the energy for the competition. I know I am superior. That is its own reward. Valerie once gloried in my gifts. Well, her. It has been quite a few years now. Worship is expected to fade. At least somewhat. That which is truly important is my confidence in myself. That never fades. I have the gift of glow.

uptown, tin ceiling in my view

Aunt Myrt lived in a big old apartment on Pleasant Avenue. Well, not that big but big rooms. One big bedroom. An almost big kitchen with a peek window onto the airshaft and a sometime breeze. And the living room, Chet's space.

She let Chet sleep on the couch. Chet, you'll be comfy there. It's a genuine horse hair. That's the very best thing for a person's back and you must maintain your posture if you're to be an actor. Just imagine. An actor in the family.

Chet hated the ancient, dark, mahogany carved horsehair couch. So hard to lie on. Might as well be on the floor. He wondered how many horses it took to stuff it. How many hundreds of years ago? Are there bugs in there too? Live bugs? And other critters?

Aunt Myrt was just so tickled to have him there. A fine child like Chester. It would be like having a son. Everything about him just made her glow. She just had to tell everyone. Everyone. And when she told Georgette down the hall, Georgette just took her by surprise.

Where you keeping that boy?
Well, what on earth do you mean? He's with me in my place.
I means, where you got him sleeping?
On my good couch.
No proper bed? For a grown man? I saw him. Six feet if he's an inch.

And Aunt Myrt went home smaller. I hear them talking all these years. My four kids this, my ten kids that, my grand-babies, my great-grand-babies and now I got Chester and that Georgette, she had to say I don't even know how to put him in a decent bed. I will not let that woman – Aunt Myrt was so consumed with anger that the thought incinerated itself before it could finish. The next day she went to the discount furniture store on Third and 122nd and bought a foldaway. She paid extra to have it delivered. Then she walked over to the 99 cent store to see if they might have any sheets in that day and Jesus smiled. They had a whole pile of perfectly good seconds in a lovely assortment of colors.

Chet thought about the total impossibility of getting his own place. Especially now that Aunt Myrt had gone and bought a foldaway just for him. Getting his own place? None of the money coming in will make that happen. Not just crunching numbers for other folks. A part-time accountant is never gonna do it. I just have too many directions to spend any money comes my way. I'm here to take classes. To make a name. But in my heart, it's always my big sister who's number one. I've got to get the money to get a proper wheelchair for Teenie. Maybe one of those souped up motor ones. Yeah. And then Teenie could cruise like she used to, all flash and curl. Now she just waves her arms. Go Chester go. Go up north and live your dream. Be my dream, little brother.

Oh, Teenie, what you couldn't do before. Before they took Cut down. A barber. A real man. But shooters are just that stupid and all red cars look red. I'm just saying. Chet remembered the way it was told. They shot Cut driving. Cut, just an innocent barber driving with his girl. Shot him cold through the neck and Teenie she tried to grab the wheel but his big dead weight foot truly dead just made the gas pedal go on pumping and the car racing into this car and that and Teenie screaming and big Cut slumped and dead and people crazy running in the street to get away from the killing car and thump and glass and the old lady flying up in the sky with her walker and then slam! at last the car goes right into the front window of Denny's and the last thing Teenie remembered was a sign for a pancake special and she never walked and never ate pancakes again.

I gotta get famous for Teenie. I gotta make money for Teenie and buy her a beautiful chair.

But first, according to Cal, I gotta watch some racy movies. How I'm gonna do that on Aunt Myrt's tv?

when i think of porn

After Victor, she grew depressed. She didn't know it was depression because she had never had this darkness descend and didn't know the name to name for it. It was a depression of urgency. She masturbated three to four times a day, sometimes more. Against the shelves in the library. Unable to stop. Leaning against the rake in between leaves. Snowball snowballing down a hill. In the girls' bathroom at middle school hidden in the far left stall. Avalanche. The vice principal caught her on the stairwell with Lowell Epps, the first boy her age she let grope hurry hurry under her shirt. The vice principal took her into his office and whispered too close, too close in her ear: Ignorance is not bliss, Wissa. Do you know where this kind of behavior will take you? She hung her eyes to her knees. He scheduled her for a remedial session at his basement apartment under Old Man Ketchum's house. No brakes.

She knew better. She knew better. She knew nothing. The depression was a speeding train. She numbed her way to his apartment buffeted by the winds whipping in the hollow of her chest. Where am I going? Afterwards, she skipped choir practice and went to the movies. Went to the movies all by herself.

A man got up and sat beside her. Put his bear claw hand on her knee. Then his hand drifted. That's a man I don't know. He could be anyone. A bum. Someone's father. A stranger's hand was so much more exciting. A stranger. He finished and got up.

Next time, wear a skirt.

She couldn't breathe for the cloud of sex crushing her. She couldn't tell her parents. She couldn't tell anyone. Where are my friends? Isn't this when you call a friend? But when she had told Lindsay about Victor, Lindsay said she should call the police and Wissa immediately knew the police would take her parents away instead. So Lindsay was off the list. The very short list. No parents to listen. How do I stop?

All these years later, she never learned.

love marriage friendship hate

After dinner, Pammy got out an old notebook and found a blank page. She had to do this. It was stage one. It gave her the right to fantasize. To build the story and fly away.

She carefully wrote: G. Calvert Blessing. And below that: Pammy Sue Kemple. It had to be your full name but all she knew was the G. It'll have to do. Every letter the two names had in common, she crossed out. An "a" for an "a." "L" for and "l" and so on. Only one for one. No cheating. Then she stared at the remaining letters and began to go from one to the other chanting, "Love marriage friendship hate." When she got to the last "e" in Kemple, the chant landed on "hate." Oh, no. That just can't be. It can't.

Well, G. is technically his first name. So what if I do just first and last names? She wrote out G. Blessing and Pammy Kemple and began crossing out the common letters one by one. Time for the chant over the letters that weren't struck out. Love marriage friendship hate love marriage friendship hate love marriage friendship hate. No! Not hate again. I have to find out what "G." stands for. I know that will make all the difference.

Okay, one last time. She wrote out Cal Blessing, then Pammy Kemple. The cross-outs went quicker this time. Love marriage friendship hate. Four times she chanted over the unstruck letters and again the ending was hate.

It's never this bad. Something is definitely wrong. I'm doing everything I can and it's not working. I'll just shut my eyes. I'll just shut my eyes.

But she couldn't shut down the urge. The urge to connect on any level however imaginary. The propulsion of thought into his life. The invisible postal touch. Yes, that's what I'll do. That idea felt good. Right. A positive step. An activity. Tomorrow I'll start looking through the backs of magazines. I'll start with Mother's stack of Good Housekeeping in the bathroom. He won't know it's me but I'll know it's me. I'll know he read something I sent him. Well, in a roundabout way. Direct would just be way too scary.

Finding a path to connection relaxed her and sleep enveloped. This time it will be perfect. I'll buy some stamps after work tomorrow. She pulled the blanket up high to her chin. Her body shifted into a comfy fetal curl. Her heart steadied into a slow determined beat.

the reality of g.

Calvert glanced down at the money order Chet had handed him on entering the loft. As usual, I will have to pray a weekly payment appears from all of them. Where are all the wealthy wannabees? He made sure the money order was made out properly as he had instructed: G. Calvert Blessing. He folded it into neat thirds as he vaguely listened to them prattle on about the challenges of their assignment.

G. Calvert Blessing. The G. stood for nothing. It was a family tradition. All the males had a G. before their name. It went back so many generations that the roots of the tradition had rotted from memory. Calvert's cousin G. Caleb Blessing had traced the family back to 1607 to the village of Bibury in England. A total obsessive-compulsive pedant, my cousin. Years he devoted to such a finite, mindless project. It was as if his scoliosis had destined him to stoop for hours over ancient church records. How he exuded positive ecstasy the day he called to announce the discovery of a G. Simon Blessing born the 8th of August, 1607 to G. Clovis Blessing and Marguerite.

Cousin G. Caleb has no children. Brother G. Winston had no children. I have no children. There. That is the end of the mindless G's.

On the other hand, when he was in an upbeat mood, Calvert preferred to think that the G. stood for god.

and we continue

Calvert listened and shook his head with exaggerated despair.

And that is all you came away with? You are all idiots. It is make believe, remember. A sheet artfully arranged here. Two mouths open there. But it is you as the audience who imagines the tongue probing. On camera, tongues look like some emerging primordial platypi. That is the plural of platypus, my zoologically undernourished friends. No tongues. Ever. And nipples. Do you know nothing of the human body?

Cal digests the looks on their faces. You are frightening them. Do not take your life with Valerie out on these possible innocents.

Chet examines his thrift shop never worn shoes. Definitely worth the investment. Got to present myself. These shoes must have been pinching some guy's fat toes. But Chet had beautiful long toes for those oh Jesus so fly brand new wingtip shoes. Perfect toes. What's this Cal so worked up over? All she asked was how do they make the nipples stand up for the camera.

Pammy sobbed. Cal walked over to her with a tissue.

Stop your weeping, my darling, and we will continue.

He sat back down on his throne. Oh, my knees are bad today.

Now, a most famous quote from that celebrated thespian, Sean Connery. Perhaps you have heard it, perhaps not. Of course, it is often attributed to others and you, gentlemen, might use it yourselves on a closed set someday to a sweet female actress. The human anatomy always has a mind of its own. The quote: "Forgive me if I get an erection. And forgive me if I don't." And there you go. Cocks rise and fall. Nipples get hard. You and your body are rarely as one.

Now, in an up and up production, they will alert you before an audition if nudity is involved or simulated sex required. No one will force you to perform. But this class will enable you to perform well. Contracts, of course, put it all in writing and you should never be without one.

Pammy wiped her nose. He knows so much. He has such a great voice. I can feel his voice inside me. This is his tissue. I'll keep it forever.

He likes to hear himself talk, thinks Seamus. I have a feeling he swings both ways. Nice socks, too. Socks are revealing.

Calvert continued. Last week, we discussed just how many crew people may be prepping or actually might be in the bedroom, the bar bathroom, the back seat of a Chevy or in the forest to prime your sexual performance. Today, I want you to learn how to be comfortable with that crew. You will relax.

George, you know how to relax. You have attended this class before. Tell them about your journey.

Classic deer in the headlights.

Hi. I'm George Gowerlich. I'm a telephone repairman and an actor.
You are an actor, George.
I'm an actor and I've had parts, done extra work in soaps and movies and, thanks to Cal, I know nobody is like me and I go in there to the auditions for principal stuff like leads and if it's me they're looking for, there I am and nobody's like me. And someday, it'll be me they're looking for.

Not exactly the answer I sought but thank you, George. In this class, as you can see, there is no crew, no camera, no eyes except ours. So, to commence, I want you to realize that any discomfort you might have about your physical appearance is meaningless. They want you there or you would not be there. They want the cellulite and the pimples and the excess hair. And if they do not, believe me, they will make it disappear. That is the magic.
Now, our exercise. Tell the class which part of your body you would or would not be comfortable exposing? Think about that further when you go home and always remind yourselves that embarrassment is meaningless. Let us start with an adult.

Cal nods at Maura.

That did not feel like a compliment. Maura sat up a little straighter, channeling her mother.

Hmmm. I think I might, I'm really not sure, but I think I might be willing to expose my breasts. But it just wouldn't be gratuitous. It would have to be for the story line.

No t & a for you, Cal muses to himself. This one interests me.

And your nipples. Might they perchance get hard?

The fucking bastard's baiting me. Without a hair of hesitation, Maura blurts out:
They get hard in the dairy section of the grocery store and I still manage to shop.

Very witty, my dear. And you, Mr. Seamus Cohen? Odd coupling, that. Someday, I hope you will indulge us in the tale of your heritage.
I'm okay with being seen. From what I see, it's usually a guy's ass they're more likely to show. So I'm okay with that.

Cal focused on Pammy shrinking in her confessional chair.

I don't think I should be naked. I mean, I have cellulite.

Cal's mind is aghast. This coming from a girl whose elbows can be classified as a weapon?

Where, might I ask?
From my thighs to my ankles. I see it every time in the mirrors in Bloomingdale's.

Nobody missed that last word. It was Wissa who spoke up.

You shop where?
Well, just for bathing suits.

Pammy was suddenly so very economically suspect. Did she have money? One more reason she's not one of us. We wear starving actors on our sleeve even if it isn't true. The code is never never reveal where you really shop. Unless you have a sugar daddy and totally flaunt it.

But Cal's mind was on a different path.

May I inquire why a young lady with cellulite from her ankles to her thighs is even shopping for a bathing suit?
Uh, Cosmopolitan Magazine—

Maura decided to save the floundering mouse.

A woman should always have a bathing suit in case someone asks her to suddenly run away for a romantic Caribbean moment.

Maura glanced at her watch. Class is halfway over. Well, thank you Pammy for taking up so much time with your shrinking subversive ways. You certainly know how to make the light shine on you.

Pammy thinks, I want to be you Maura. So calm. So sure.

Cal's eyes settle on Bibi.

Moving on, class. You with the beautiful hair.

Every part of me's been seen. Why am I here? I could be on this new goddamned internet for all I know. That man one day with the buzzy camera. Another one of Papi Fannon's buddies. Bibi, Bibi, remember you here to put it behind. To see how it scares them and don't scare me. That I know it back and up and round and here I am. Wait, that's what this Cal just said. It go nowhere. The fear, the shame it count for nothing. Here I am.

I don't like my legs. I have big calves.
Now there is an honest young woman. All of you focus on so-called privates and she sees the big picture. The wide angle lens. I am positively smitten.

clock times out

Cal almost wished he were stoned. This is so much fun watching them squirm. How even more delicious it would be were I on another level entirely. But he had closed that door decisively. I am much too prone to navel gazing when artificially elevated. I would much rather gaze at another's.

Do not think you have gotten away so easily, my little ones – and big ones. We have another exercise. Now that we know what parts of your bodies you would prefer to hide, we are going to have an exercise in exposure. I want you to remove one piece of clothing. Just one. You must, however, remove it with all the seductive power at your disposal. You may look at one of your classmates if that is a help. Or, you may direct your eyes to a distant fixed point, to the imaginary. Do not, I beg, look at me. You will get no extra credit for arousing your teacher.

Only George laughed. He remembered to laugh from last semester. But that time everybody laughed. Today it was just George. The rest of the class was too consumed in choosing which part of their attire to discard. It felt like a critical decision. Life or death. Calvert watched their wheels turn. Nobody laughed at my joke.

Nobody laughed. Well, George did. But George has been trained. I cannot imagine what metamorphosis he was expecting by enrolling again. I am delighted, though, to take your money once more. Thank you, George.

No volunteers? Very well, Willa you shall go first.
My name is—
No verbiage. Movement.

Legs crossed, Wissa leaned over very slowly, her back a creamy curve. She took her right sneaker shoelace between her fingers. Looking up into Anton's eyes the entire time, she pulled the bow open, then lowered her head even further to put one shoelace in her mouth. Keeping it taut with her hands, she began to fellate the shoelace in an alarmingly innocent way, as if she were just thirsty.

You can stop now. I will assume your ultimate goal was to remove your shoe. I am sorry to say, we will not have sufficient time for everyone to do this exercise. Perhaps one more, though. Anton?

Anton stood up. Everyone had to look up at him. He pulled at the fake gold of his expandable watch band. He pulled it as wide as it would go and then let it snap back against his wrist. He slid the watch from his hand and dropped it into the thick of his palm. Then he looked up and locked eyes with Maura. He walked towards her. Stopped. He opened his hand revealing the sacrificial watch.

Cal clapped. He hadn't clapped for Wissa. Everyone else in the class registered that immediately and their respective muscles froze. Cal's smile faded.

And the clock says "go." Your homework this week is to view professional pornography versus the simulated sex you studied last week. Believe me, reality is present in neither. You may rent videos or, for those of you with computers, I understand there is a plethora of material to choose from on the internet.

Did I truly say "I understand?" How could you possibly feign humble innocence of your favorite playground? What else do you do while Valerie is out working? Besides my lovely soap carvings, it is whack whack whack.

Just then, Valerie slipped in, emerging from the stairwell, wearing giant tribal earrings and her corporate money suit. She glided almost silently across to the living area and didn't quite close the door behind her.

Oh, she is home early. And I was so hoping to have a certain teacher to student tête-à-tête.

Well, there you go, my actors. Be off and prosper.

They scrambled out of the loft. Wissa lingered.

I got it. I got the commercial. The young mom I told you about last week.
Oh, very impressive. Do not, however, forget Marilyn Chambers.

Wissa's face registered zero.
Valerie listened by the door opening to the private part of the loft.

Before your time. Very well, dear Willa, I must tell you about her.
It's Wissa.
Regardless, Marilyn Chambers had the face of purity. They pictured her on all the sweet boxes of Ivory Snow. She had a cherubic baby at her breast. Then, when acting jobs were scarce, she took that golden face and spread her legs on screen. A pornographic pioneer in her day. Our paths did cross – before her notoriety, that is.

Valerie ducked back behind the door.

My point: enjoy being a young mom. You never know where it will take you.
Oh. Thank you.
Goodbye, little one.

Wissa managed a shrug goodbye, not quite sure of Cal's implications.

Cal saw Valerie's hand reach out to leave a note on their door. His curiosity about the note lengthened his strides. He read: "Don't open that door too wide. Particularly, the green one." His lips curled downward. You, Valerie, are a true spoilsport.

valerie

More and more I wonder what on earth I'm doing with this man. Didn't Mama cast a dark eye on him? You have degrees. We sent you to college. You will do everything I was denied in my suburban sacrifice all for your father life. You will have your own bank account.

I do have my own bank account. I did even then at Chumley's that night. Me and Poochee having a drink after that play at The Cherry Lane. The unmarked door. The coolest, scariest door-step we'd ever crossed. He was there. He was next to me at the bar. And then Cal kissed her behind her ear and whispered in his actor voice.

Valerie remembered when he was the best of wild she needed. And, of course, in business it gave her an added cachet to have a husband in the arts. In the Arts. It made her seem more worldly, Bohemian. She thought it made her seem more worldly, Bohemian. She became known for her big, bold jewelry. Heavy silver garnished with massive stones. No pink-bowed tight neck blouses for her under her suits. No. A simple black suit from Lord & Taylor adorned with look-at-me-I-have-a-husband-in-the-Arts jewelry glistening as I analyze, theorize, forecast the stimulating world of commodities futures.

But now I know Valerie Blessing is a fraud. A fraud with no future. I knew Cal was a fraud first. And now I look at him and see only me. Wretched in this loft. Stuck here forever because it's rent-controlled in nyc. And the landlord, the landlord would kick us out onetwothree if she ever knew we tore down walls years ago to make it more hip, even more loft-like. But still, I can't breathe even if the windows are wide. Doors locked but nothing stays out. In New York you can always hear the movement outside, the sound of traffic, the hum of millions of air conditioners, the diesel bracing horns of the big trucks, sirens, the shouts of drunken kids at 3:00 a.m. Someone is always moving, moving in the city. And Cal and I? Like those old jungle movies with the quicksand. We're sinking.

your everyday subway night

Wissa went through the turnstile and saw George further down the platform. Not easily missed. That big globby body. Hairy arms hanging out of those awful plaid short sleeve shirts. It's winter. Where's your coat? Or is it his permanent collection of calories that keeps him warm? She felt obligated to join him, her classmate. George smiled at her blondness. She's so clean.

Hi George.

Silence and then: So, do you have parents?

Is he really asking me that question?

Yeah.
Do you like them?

Is he crazy? Who asks that?

Yeah.
What do they do?
Well, my Dad is a carpenter and my Mom's a—a beautician.

Like hair?
Well, actually she's an eyebrow specialist, really.
They have special people like that for dead people.

Wissa took a quick look around for something, someone to grab onto in case George pushed her onto the subway tracks.

You know, special people like in the funeral homes to like make them up and do eyebrows and hair. I guess if maybe they were missing eyebrows or— Does your Mom work on dead guys?
No. That would be too weird.
Yeah, I guess. But an interesting job. They can't complain. But I guess they don't tip.

The train pulled in. Wissa didn't move.

I think I'm going to wait for the local. Gets me closer to the crosstown bus.

George waved goodbye.

I should have known. I'm taking a class like this. All that twirling with his stringy beard creeps me out. But he asked me about my parents. How many guys ask me anything about me? Talk talk about themselves but zero curiosity about Wissa beyond the size of my tits and the color of my bush. George was curious. In a creepy way. The way that usually makes me lie.

Lately, I've been wondering if any of my lies are really lies. Is reinvention pure fiction? Like with my Mom. Maybe it's just memories side by side, never touching. Parallel worlds and all that. On the phone this month, Wissa brought it all up again with her Mom and she flat out said they never talked about such a thing and where does she get her crazy ideas. You've been like that since you were a child. Maybe my reality is not true. After all, Mom's so positive about what she remembers. Maybe everything is in flux and all memories are just what you think at the moment. Maybe that's why so many of those guys looked right through me like we never slept together, never fucked together, never sweat spit slapped skin together. Maybe their reality never included me.

How do I get them out of mine?

touch

Seamus saw Bibi up ahead. Head hunched, hair wild, back to him. His route was a left at the corner. She made a right. Seamus scurried to catch up with her.

Wait. Bibi, you know I write, freelance. It's how I pay the rent. Would you like to come to dinner on my tab? Maybe later this week. I have to review a new Cuban restaurant in the Village and I can bring someone as my guest.
I'm not Cuban.
Neither am I.
But you thinking 'cause I'm a Latina, I'm gonna know what's the right food to eat. Maybe translate the menu for you as some kind of bonus?
What's with the defensive? I just thought I'd ask so we can both have a free meal. Maybe have some fun.

Once again he attempted to pass her a simple business card with his name and number printed in a basic adult courier font. He was trying so hard to be an adult.

Why don't you take my number this time? You know, you just talked completely differently than you do in class. I listen. I notice.

I was angry.
Hey, it's just food.

Bibi stared at his pale freckled outstretched hand. She took the card.

Seamus's brain fell into a shambles of propriety. I should leave first. Can't walk her to the train where she's probably heading. Already, I know that's a bad move. Bibi for sure is a person you can't push. So many walls. What is it about her that's already inside me? Will she call? Am I that bad? It's not like it's a date. I should have asked Wissa, even Maura. Everybody likes a free meal. But I just have a feeling. Please call, Bibi.

When she got down into the subway, Bibi rummaged around her bag for an old receipt, anything to spit her gum into. She came up empty handed. She used Seamus's card but carefully folded it and put it back in her purse.

maura at home

It isn't much of a class. Maybe the whole point is just to think. I'm certainly thinking. Thinking about cellulite from my hips to my ankles. Maybe not Pammy's dimensions but definitely mine. And that's not a figment of a paranoid imagination. Wrinkly knees. Saggy elbows. It's one thing to have a colonoscopy test and feel the calendar moving but this older woman body is glued to me. No escape. Naked on camera? Me? Don't think that's about to happen any time soon and doubt anyone's aching to ask.

Perhaps it's really a group therapy that we've all stumbled into and that Calvert is running. Some secretive clinical trial for a mystery psychotropic drug. Maybe there are hidden cameras registering our remarks and facial expressions. Maybe Calvert doesn't even know he's doing this. Perhaps there really is a wizard behind the curtain. His wife? That big woman who kind of quietly strides past the class with all that enormous jewelry? Wonder what she does. Art gallery maybe. Museum? Therapist? Maybe we'll all drink Kool-Aid and curl up nighty-night on his threadbare old rug. Gus would laugh.

Why am I thinking about Gus? Yeah, well, pornography, dodo. Our homework. Maybe it just titillates that old fart to see the kids take his commands, his pronouncements, as gold. He's not much older than you, Maura.

Oh, Gus. You, my love, will never get old. Pornography. Gus. Pornography. Gus. Happy together. Even so close to dying when you decided spur of the moment to hop a plane and say goodbye to your Mom in Phoenix and they removed the sick passenger from the plane. Gus, the sick passenger sweating salty silent screams wracked with sickle cell pain. And days later, he appeared back at the apartment never even telling me he'd been in the hospital. He just went to bed. You just collapsed on the bed. And then I saw the patient bracelet on your arm. And all that time, I'd thought you'd been in Phoenix. Don't you even have my name somewhere in that cracked leather wallet to contact in case of emergency? We're married.

I unpacked his small duffel. A toothbrush loose with no cover. One pair of jockey shorts. One sock. Two t-shirts. Five porn magazines. All blonds. Always blonds.

No blond here.

I asked him. I asked him later why he would bring all those magazines to his Mom's house. He looked at me. The look. How many times did I shrink, withered by his strange disdain?

"Well, I'm not about to pack a video."

Enough memories. He was. I am. And I loved him. In spite – in spite of it all. Oh, how he did love women. How could I not love him? The connoisseur chose me as number one.

The assignment, Maura. Professional pornography. Well, I still have Gus's collection. I know them all by heart. No. Let's go into new territory. Territory that barely existed when he was alive. She opened up the computer and explored.

under flannel sheets single bed

Pammy's mind went this way and that. She wondered what she would pack for her weekend with Cal in Aruba. That's where he would invite her to run away. The deserts of Aruba. Someone—who was it? Someone had told her there were deserts in Aruba. Are they sand deserts? She remembered being so surprised that there were other types of deserts with brush and bush and thorns and rocks and trees and cacti. All she ever imagined was endless sand. Drifting dunes waving heat lines squiggly into the sky.

Get back to the story. Before Cal takes me into the hotel room with the big bed and all windows overlooking the sea – does the desert lead straight into the sea? I'll pack the brown cotton pants and my black-eyed lazy susan dress and my new black bathing suit from Bloomingdale's with the beige cover-up. Is that enough for a weekend? I hate my bathing suit. It has too many straps and I can't fill up the bra cups right. I shouldn't have bought it. It was too much money and I have no ass.

Maybe the moment we step off the plane or before we leave, Cal will hand me some money to buy some new things. He's a famous actor. Well, not that famous I'm beginning to think. But famous enough to hand me some money. He's got to have lots of money. Yes, that's what he'll do. Here Pammy, some extra funds to spruce up your wardrobe for our little getaway. Our little getaway under the sun, drinking drinks with floaty umbrellas and resting in hammocks and sunsets and arms and legs.

Her hand was growing tired. You know if you think about clothes and stuff, you'll never reach that smile place. Concentrate, Pammy. Move your hips. Don't just be flat on the bed. Think about Cal sucking on your nipples. I always like my nipples. I like feeling them go hard. But I don't even own any sexy underwear. I only have training bras. What am I in training for? Maybe he could – maybe he'll buy me......

The fantasy ended in sleep. No smile tonight.

bibi in other worlds

In my dreams, I remember the powers I used to have. I remember the trees on the day Mami took me all the way up to Inwood Park. So many trees I felt the green fill up the air, stamp its color on my lungs. I be seeing a green crown on Mami's head making her so beautiful. When we got home, I thought I knew how to walk on the tops of those trees. I knew I could easy be doing that in my bare feet and it would be the softest rug ever. In my dreams, even now, I remember how to walk on the tops of trees. I feel the leaves tickle between my toes.

I love that dream. I wish it would be visiting me more often. It was when I still loved Mami and thought the dark was only Papi Fannon's fault. Come back dream.

and the wheels turn

Moneymoneymoneymoney. That is freedom. My freedom. She will never die. The lovely Valerie; healthy as the proverbial horse. And luck? I have never put much weight on luck. A lottery ticket does not have my name on it.

Calvert stared at the old metal milk crate full of cheap head-shots from current and past students. The bargain headshots with bad lighting, too much make-up, too little make-up. The boys in James Dean leather jackets. The girls flashing too much cleavage. Awful wardrobe choices. Ridiculous "creative" poses. Even that Pammy mouse wasted good money. She would have been better off clipping the photograph from her high school yearbook. That mouse. All bones. Oh god, I could lift her by her clavicles.

Moneymoneymoneymoney.

But that girl, Willa. The blond. And Bibi, so juicy. Do not be ridiculous, Calvert. You would never do that. Preposterous. I bide my time and someday, by death or divorce, I shall be free. But for now, my needs are few.

He reached into the milk crate and rifled through the photos. He picked out headshots of two girls not in the current class. They were both sultry brunettes, full-lipped. He carried the pictures over to the big chair, picking up a box of tissues along the way. He sat down and carefully unzipped his fly.

where and how

Anton lived uptown in the basement of a building on Edgemont Avenue. It was a hodgepodge of little rooms, each one barely big enough to put a cot in. There were two squeezed up toilets this way and that and a separate shower that no one took responsibility to clean. Twice a year clogged up hair would dam up the water drain. Floor floods. The super, Ruben, angry to play plumber mopped and opened it up. Next to the shower was a separate ancient old claw foot bathtub, curved and ornate. The super kept various industrial supplies stacked up in it. At the end of the hall, obstructed by the building's new water heater, Anton discovered part of an old curved wooden bar. Ruben told him this basement was once a whorehouse in the thirties. Maybe that was the bar. Yes, that was the bar. Anton could see the jazzy ladies with feathers and the men in hats one foot up on the brass rail long gone and sold for cash.

Anton and Piotr were the only two Poles in the basement. All the other men were from somewhere in Africa and he would hear their voices murmuring in something almost like French. Piotr spoke some French. He told Anton some of the Africans loudest arguments were about who was the better baker. Some were cab drivers but the bakers were the royalty of the basement. Nobody cooked down there anymore. A few of the men had had hot plates in their little cubicles. The stews smelled so good late at night. But one day the super Ruben stole all the hot plates. He said it was a fire hazard. They were all a fire hazard.

The basement men hardly ever saw the other tenants in the building. The legal tenants had a separate entrance just around the corner on 157th Street. Anton once saw a girl who reminded him of his sister Ewa even though she was black. It was something about her neck and her tilting shoulder and the two braids curled up and up. Thick braids. He always wanted to touch the beautiful black girl's braids. But he'd have to speak with her first and he never did.

At night, some of the other men whispered in another African language that took Anton back to Poland to the forest near his village. He would play in the thick of the forest and stay deep into nightfall. His Mama would get so angry. Anton's dreams lingered in those memories, smelled the musk of the earth, the sounds dancing under and over. The sounds most of all. Eyes shut, this other language filled his ears like the sound of a Polish forest night. The brook. A coo. The crack crack of a twig from a passing animal. Anton would wake the next morning confused, positive his sweat was the crisp morning dew.

How am I being renting pornography? There is no television. No computer. He asked Momo:

You know where I can to see pornography?

Momo roared. He thought this the funniest thing and called over Top, the baker, the best baker. Top laughed the big laugh and pulled Anton close with his great, strong arm.

Come. Come with me.

audition for perdition

Maura found this site on the internet, Tunnel 69. They were almost like coming attractions. Snippets of films. Busts. Cum. Asses. Everything broken down into precise categories. Sweet young things. Big tits. Black white. White black. Stewardesses. Horny nurses. Older women younger men.

She clicked on that. A blond muscle guy was curled up sleeping. A plump sixty-something tired old woman comes in the room with a pile of folded laundry.

What is she supposed to be? His mother? The landlady? The maid?

The tired woman stares at the sleeping hunk then sits down on the edge of the bed, unzips his fly and begins giving him a hand job. He doesn't wake up. She goes down on him. He still doesn't wake up. Maura clicked it off. What is he, dead?

Maura saw another category: audition tapes. Well, that seems appropriate for Cal's homework. She opened the first one on the list. A striking Hispanic girl stood awkwardly in front of the camera.

She was wearing a frilly deep fuchsia top and blue jeans. Her hair fell in careful Botticelli curls down past her shoulders. Did she get up early that morning to curl her hair? Was her wardrobe a time-consuming decision of the night before? One hand kept going up to push her long hair from falling onto her face even when it wasn't there. A soft, high-pitched man's voice comes from off camera.

How old are you?
I'm nineteen.
Are you comfortable? Why are you here today?
Uh, I thought this would maybe be a good way to make some money. I saw the ad.
Do you have a boyfriend? Does he know?
No, he don't know.

She giggles.

But I guess he'll know.
Guess he will. Especially when you bring home the money once the producers see you. And you are very pretty. Very pretty. But you know that. How about you take off your shirt?

She does.

Now your bra and panties.
All of it? Do I have to?
Of course. My, you're a very tiny girl. Turn around. Show us your ass. Lift your arms. Nice. You take direction well. Producers like that. They pay a lot of money for that.
They do?
Why don't you sit on the couch there. Let me adjust the light.

Maura could tell it was just the two of them in a very small space. An office? Bland walls. Not a single picture. Beige couch with worn stained armrests.

Why don't you lay on down? Get comfortable.

The girl lies on the couch.

Spread your legs. Nice pussy.
The girl giggles again.
Thanks.
How about you masturbate for me? Do you masturbate at home?
I didn't think I'd have to—
The producers will want to see how you look sexy. You know how to masturbate, don't you? With your hands. The real thing. No dildos. No toys.
Yeah, but—
Hurry up. Let me see.

She begins. Her eyes shut. Gradually her body responds. Her eyes open, then quickly seal, avoiding his gaze, returning to her own fantasy. He brings her back.

Hmm. That pussy is looking so good. You know, for me to sell you to the producers, they're going to have to see more than this.
Well, I thought maybe I would just do, you know, like girl on girl. I could maybe call my cousin. We sometimes, you know, but just once—
Nah, some other time, baby. For the producers, I got to show them something now. What's really important is showing them

you'll go the distance. There's plenty of girls just waiting. I have to show the producers you're worth the money. There's a lot of money to be made. You need money, don't you?
She giggles.
Who don't?
Well, why don't I just play with your pussy a bit?
I guess....

He adjusts the camera. The picture goes all over the place. The ceiling, the floor and settles back on the couch but from a different angle. Thick hands enter the shot carrying a single light on a wobbly stand. The thick hands belong to a pear-shaped pale guy with greasy dirty blond hair gathered in an anorexic ponytail. This is the guy. This is the creepy sibilant voice. He carefully avoids getting his face on camera. He places the light just off frame to the right. He gets on his knees by the couch. He fingers her. Then he goes down on her. She gets into it or fakes it. Maura isn't sure which is the case.

He gets up.

We'll have to show them you can suck cock. Everybody in the business sucks cock. You can't demand just girl on girl till you're a big star. I'll make you a big star. You suck your boyfriend's cock. I bet you do. Show me how.
But....

She does. His stubby fingers encircle her skull. His flesh, the pale grayish color of skim milk, ripples towards her face. A sweaty sheen coats his skin. Just watching, Maura could smell the clammy humidity rising off his boneless flesh. Bet no one sprayed him with glycerin. He reaches down, grabs the young girl by the hips, spins her and pushes her back on the couch. Barely a second and he's fucking her from behind.

You're going to make a lot of money, baby. A lot of money.

With a jerky thrust of his ass, he comes and then pulls out of her. He walks out of the picture.

I hope you're taking the pill or something.
I guess...

The girl stands back up and looks a little lost, now solo in front of the camera again.
The man's soft voice intrudes from off screen.

That was easy, wasn't it? What'd you think?
Well...

She no longer looks directly at the camera. She looks at her hands.

I didn't think I'd be naked today. I mean I did but— I maybe should have put on some more lotion— My skin looks kind of ashy, you know.
Nah. You look good.

And then the tape ended abruptly.

Maura turned off the computer. She kept thinking how worried the girl was about not putting on enough lotion so her skin wouldn't look ashy. How could she be thinking of that and not the fact that that fat bozo had just fucked her and come inside her? For free. No protection. Zero. An audition tape auditioning for nothing except probably his cheap thrill and now everyone could see it on the computer and her boyfriend probably left her or beat her or worse. Was she just a stupid, stupid little duped girl?

Maura felt so depressed about it, guilty for watching this girl be so money craving stupid and get taken advantage of. "I hope you're taking the pill or something," he said. Asshole pig. Sad duped teenager.

And she remembered looking at those ads once in the back of The Village Voice. Models wanted. Adult actress needed. Did I not think of applying? Did I not imagine taking off my clothes? Would I have let it keep going beyond where I thought the audition should go? Yeah, I would have taken my clothes off—but sex? Sex is for the fantasy of the audition, not the reality. It was her reality. That girl's reality. Where is she now? Maybe she put it all behind her and never went there in her head again. Maybe she does have an illustrious adult film career. Maybe she got her boobs done and dyed her hair red. Maybe she's sad and totally alone. Thin and alone with her tiny waist. Maybe she got fat in the middle and that audition turned into a pregnancy. Her questioning boyfriend and a suspect pale baby with blondish hair. Whose baby is this? All hell. Fire and brimstone.

Maura got up from the desk. She could feel the moistness in her underpants. Oh my God, I'm wet.

She rarely drank by herself at home. She pulled out spices and cans of soup to reach the few liquor bottles in the back of the kitchen cabinet. She poured a shot of tequila and then another and only later remembered salt and lemon would have been a nice addition. By then, though, she was stumbling to sleep.

flopping on the foldaway

Dear Teenie,

Life at Aunt Myrt's is pretty much the same. Wrote you about her getting a foldaway. Way better in zzzz-land. And class

Chet stopped writing, letting the sentence hang mid-air. Class. So my homework is to watch real porn. Well, it ain't gonna happen here. I guess I could get a magazine but that wasn't Cal's intent I know. I've got a good imagination. I'll use that imagination.

He switched off the lamp on the side table and let his eyes close. He loved how his eyes felt warm when they were shut. How perfectly they fit together. Think my eyes are happier that way. Who'll I'll think of? That girl in the laundry room? The one with the flat tits. She looked at me. I know the type of tits she had. Big and flat against her chest. The type some skinny girls get and black black around her nipples. Oh shit. I gotta get up early to iron that shirt for that audition for that music video. Will they notice I'm not a professional dancer? I mean the notice just said male dancers. Concentrate. I'm touching her tits. She's making an oh baby noise. She's slithering down my chest with her nipples hard on me. I gotta remember my posture at the audition. I gotta look sharp. I don't even feel like doing this. Maybe there's some of Aunt Myrt's buttermilk pie left in the fridge.

scars my shadow

Wissa remembered the breaking of the glass. The blue jar hitting the bathroom floor. The deep cuts that stared at her with no pain and then slowly filled with blood. The lack of time. Total absence. The internal command: make the outside as ugly as within.

How dumb I was to hate that girl. I was just too young. Too young for everything that was drowning me. Gloom and doom and empty awful sex. Look at me now, you dark cloud teenager. Look at me now. I'm going everywhere. I'm waking up tomorrow and going to that studio on West 56th and I'm going to look right into that camera and say, "I'm never going back to those old diapers again."

I have everything ahead and still she tags along. She's forever on my arms, letting everyone know of her existence. I can't shed her like fat. I can't shed her ever.

She shut her eyes and, for a moment, thought she smelled fresh cut wood. The barn was always filled with music. Audio was a prime concern for Dad and he even consulted with his friend Mel, the garage band king. Wow. I almost forgot that whole thing.

Mel had grown up with Dad except Mel, with some success, had managed to not really grow up. He put it together from band to band. He even lived in a garage. And the band kids kept getting younger and Mel, older. And then, just like some magic door being opened, the early gray hairs foresting his head made him into some kind of garage band guru. To play with Mel became an honor, a rite of local rock and roll passage. To listen to him play commanded the best drugs available. And you needed to be high. After all, he was still Mel, a forty-eight year old aspiring garage band musician.

With Mel's advice, large two foot speakers hung from the ceiling, looming dark like road kill ravens resurrected. Three smaller speakers clung to the barn's support beams. Joan Baez sang her Daddy was a handsome devil. "Maggie May" hoarsely echoed in the big space. "Sweet Baby James." "Misty Roses." "Molly." The hippie Muzak loop filled her head. Album after album round and round on the KLH record player. She always knew exactly what song followed each cut. But this was her parents' music. Wissa saved money to buy cassettes and she longed for a Walkman CD player like all the other girls had. But I'm not like the other girls. The dark thoughts expanded daily. It was months after Victor and all sorts of things were bubbling up inside. All sorts of things. None of them good.

She heard the screen door open. Mom was back from the Rexall. Wissa ambled down the stairs. She'd been staring at the photos more and more. The small ones on the fridge. The framed ones along the length of the stairs. Mom and Dad. Me. Mom and Dad. Me. Me and Mom. Mom and Dad.

Mom was unpacking the Rexall bag on the kitchen table. She handed Wissa a box of tampons and kept another one for herself. She pulled out a bottle of cola syrup for her upsets. Wissa spotted what she was really interested in. Mom dropped the packet of developed photos on the table. Wissa flipped through them. Who was in the pictures and who was not? The random configurations not random at all. The Labor Day bonfire and cookout. Victor's birthday party. Her parents' anniversary. Her and Mom.

Which ones do you think? The fridge is getting crowded.
Mom, I want to ask you. Please don't get mad. It's just something I've been thinking over and over and things don't feel right.
Is Dad—is Dad really my father?
What kind of question is that?
Is he really?
Every kid goes through a phase where they think they're adopted. You're just heading big time into your teenage years. It's all hormones, Wissa. So, no. We're the only parents you've ever had. No adoption, honey.
I'm not asking if I was adopted.

It was some moment of hesitation. The slight inhale. Without words, she knew.

Who's my real father? Does he know I exist?

Her mother sat down slumped down into the Dad-carved oak chair. She looked at her hands for crib notes but there were none. Totally unprepared for this test.

He knows you exist. He doesn't know he's your father.
Who—?

Her mother grabbed her hard by the wrist. Bruising hard.

He doesn't know. And you won't know. And you won't speculate or talk or brood about this. You have a nice life. Look at this house. Your Dad made it. And you have nice things and —

She twisted Wissa's hand into pain.

And I won't have you messing up my life. I won't have you do this. Out of here. Now. And when you come back for dinner, we never had this conversation. Never.

It was a walk out without even a slamming door. Maybe somewhere in her heart the door slammed but her feet were too leaden and her arms fell heavy against her sides. She was in the yard. She saw the Duggan's house to the right and the Losavia's to the left and then a slippery fear trickled in and she ran, ran to beach and blue ocean and cried.

Go away. Go away. I don't want those thoughts. I need to bring up the smile. Act happy, Wissa. I'm waking up tomorrow happy and going to that studio on West 56th happy and I'm going to look right into that camera happy and say, "I'm never going back to those old diapers again."

mr. cruise

Seamus had a sometime crush on Tom Cruise. Not the current Tom Cruise but the Tom Cruise in "Risky Business," forever young, forever sliding around in white boxer shorts. He imagined his cock sliding back and forth take after take. It's crazy. I know it's crazy to pine after someone I don't know, will never know but deep inside, deep inside I do know we would click if we met. Who cares if he's gay or straight? How do I get to move in his circle? Certainly I'm not going to dip into scientology, nice Jewish boy that I am – but something social? A charity event? Like I have money for a charity gala. I am a charity gala.

Oddly, it was a crush he had cultivated. That didn't even come naturally to him. It wasn't even his real crush but that one was so secret he hardly ever let himself go there in his head. But this one, Tom Cruise, it had become a habit and easy, a sexual comfort food.

But what if I got a day as an extra on one of his films? And our eyes lock and later a production assistant comes by listening to something on her walkie and it was "Please bring that one to my trailer." And yeah, that one is this one. Me. "Mr. Cruise would like a moment with you." And that moment is me with his cock in my mouth and it's the best blow job he ever had and he can't live without me. Or there's a headline in some tabloid that he frequented The Ramble. That would get me there. I wouldn't be afraid then. I'd just go. Especially if he might be there.

Seamus, oh Seamus. Who rents "Risky Business" when the assignment is porn?

Seamus looked around the video store. He didn't have a clue if they had real porn here. Is that legal? Of course it is, ninny. Yeah, I could go over to 8th Avenue and peep or buy but here I can rent. That is, if they have any. I like this store. It's very mom and pop except it's all pop. Support your local merchant. Seamus was a firm believer.

He wandered over to the drama section. That guy with the big shoulders in the college professor sport coat. He was just here. Where did he go?

Then Seamus saw a flash of olive green, saw that wide wale corduroy coat slip through a curtain to the back room of the store. A small sign was taped to the curtain: Adults Only. Seamus sent his feet in that direction. Nature calls. Postpone Cal's assignment. Or maybe this is the assignment.

He made a beeline for the curtain. It just felt hot. And he liked it even if it was only eye contact and it usually was. He had a last fleeting thought for the Tom Cruise white boxer shorts. He couldn't remember a sex scene. Just imagination.

pass fail for effort

The candy store was all she could think of. Pammy stopped in on her way home from work. It was right by the subway stop with racks of newspapers out front. Newspapers in so many languages it made the neighborhood feel like a globe to her. She squeezed inside past a heavy man with a thick mustache. He was barking numbers at the owner, clutching lottery ticket stubs. The owner was punching numbers into a machine.

They have no eyes for me. I can do this here. Professional pornography. Calvert didn't really say it had to be movies. At least, I don't think he did. So maybe I can find a magazine and maybe they might have a short story in it or something that I can read.

Pammy edged past the fashion glossies, Popular Mechanics and the sports magazines. Right up above was the section she barely dared to look at. Big Tits. Girl Gallery. Maximum Ass. She took a quick glance over her shoulder. Lottery man and the owner were still doing business. Her thin hand reached up for Girl Gallery. A blond wearing a big hat held a watering can strategically over her breasts. She was surrounded by daisies.

The sound of the door opening jarred her. A teenage boy waved to the owner and ambled toward the soda case. The store was so narrow that his hip brushed hers. He sees me. He sees what I'm about to buy. They'll all see.

Pammy scurried out of the store. I'll fail. How can Calvert love me if I fail?

not the face of a stranger

Thick maroon velvet curtains created a second door against the chill of the wind. The whole restaurant was drowning in maroon. Maroon brocade banquettes, maroon tiles, maroon wall hangings. He expected the promised genuine Cuban house musicians to be fully clad in maroon and strumming maroon painted guitars.

I can fly with this one. An easy review barely a menu required. I can just relax and enjoy the food. I've got my interior decorating lead already. I wish I had her eyes. Her iris as black as her pupil. Bibi's eyes were downcast now, carefully fixed on her silverware, occasionally on the sweet roll untouched on her butter plate.

Where were you brought up?
New York.
New York's five boroughs. Miles and miles.
New York.
Okay. Let's try another one. We might even make it to dessert. I have a gut feeling you and I might be alike in some ways. Do you have a lot of friends? Or maybe just a best friend?

Bibi's eyes left the roll and seared into Seamus's.

You see me as some kind of popularity queen? I don't gotta answer no questions.
There you go again. Angry grammar versus — versus what? Do you even realize when you switch back and forth?

I look at him. This is a nice boy. Educated like the Professor. Be calm. Be a lady. Bibi he asked you here. He reached out his skinny white hand. Like the Professor. Like the Professor. He sees you. Got eyes for nobody else in this restaurant.

Bibi, I'm not your enemy. This is how you find out who someone is. Tell you what. Ask me something. Anything. Ask.

Bibi looked away from Seamus. This was a mistake. Unfolding that stupid business card with all the gum on it was a mistake. Not going straight home after work was a mistake. Waiting for the Professor to save me was a mistake. Seamus's quiet words invaded her head whorl. But something about this Seamus guy is different from them all. Even the Professor.

Seamus volunteered: Okay then, I'll answer the question you haven't asked me in return. I don't have any friends, well, right now. Like real ones.

Do men talk like that? To me? Then the words slipped out before she could discipline them.

I ain't never. I haven't ever had friends. Not really either.
We're talking.

A suggestion of a smile moved her lips, the upper slightly fuller than the lower.

Well, I have to go.
Wait, we haven't even had the entrées.
I just can't.
Okay then. At least give me your phone number this time. Let's make this a two way street.

Bibi wrote her number on a crumpled Dunkin' Donuts receipt she found in her black pleather shoulder bag. Seamus reached across the table but Bibi pulled back and tore it up.

Not fair. Do I have to give you another one of my business cards first? I showed you mine. You show me yours.

Bibi winced. Her face filled every inch of his focus and he saw pain.

I'm sorry. What did I say? I was just trying to be witty.

He got up and sat beside her on the banquette. He put his arm protectively around her. Oh Dios mio. How long it been since somebody done that? In a good way. Like this good way. The pressure of his hand on her shoulder relaxed her. I feel like some baby wrapped all tight. Somebody else's baby. Not me.

You okay? I'm not sure what I said but the look on your face.
I'm okay.

Seamus dropped his arm. Her body immediately missed his warmth. Her basic blank expression returned to her face but she rummaged in her purse again and came up with another random receipt to write on.

Here.

playing hooky

Mother never allowed her to miss a day of school unless she was sick with fever over a hundred and here she was deliberately skipping a day of work. Everything inside was shaky. What if someone from work sees her? No, they're at work. Well, what if when I come back tomorrow and they don't think I look sick enough? No one even looks at me. Well, maybe once.

Pammy hugged the afternoon shadow of the spindly gingko tree across from Cal's building. She had used the bathrooms in three diners before she got here. Drinking coffee to pass the time and then getting the runs. But I'm here. I just want to see him come out of the building. See where he goes. See what he does in his real life when he's not our teacher. Maybe follow him to an audition. See what kind of coat he wears. Maybe he wears a hat. Oh yes, one with a brim. So distinguished. It would go with his voice.

Maybe Calvert sees the actress in me. Sees the woman in me and some of his mean things, the mean things he says are just to cover up that he really likes me.

It's not like I've never acted before. Well, not really but I tried. I made the effort. Laura had touched something in her. Little in her life reflected "The Glass Menagerie." Everything in the feel of her life mirrored it. I can see her. I know her. I can smell the apartment she lived in. I knew her enough to put my name on the list for the tryouts junior year. But the drama teacher, Mrs. Azarac, said Pammy was over-acting when she was just being herself. "Just be yourself," gray, prune-faced Mrs. Azarac urged. This is myself. Can't you hear me screaming? But the words were within and the part was given to one of the popular girls.

I was being myself. It's not good enough. It's nothing. Boxed in, locked in, unable to find a door into any conversation, hurrying home one day two days every day to Mother. Of course, fantasy began to fill the in-between of her days. Even now. Even at work. I am my own lifeguard.

Pammy was a receptionist at a talent agency and even though most of the business was done on the phone, sometimes big names came into the office in person. It was her job to offer coffee or tea. Once, this famous actor – she couldn't even say his name inside her head the memory hurt so much – this famous actor came into the office. She had heard his voice over the phone so many, many times. She felt she knew him. He walked in all gorgeous and scruff and she said "Hello Harry" instead of calling him mister or sir. But he grinned this magic lopsided grin. She thought that meant he loved her immediately. That was the positive fantasy. Negative = his look was so squinched, maybe it was displeasure at her being so Hollywood familiar. Neutral = he had gas. All Pammy fantasies instantaneously had positive, negative and neutral takes. That's what kept her balanced. That's what keeps me balanced. I will never go off the deep end. I can't. How could I? No one would be there to catch me. Mother never could. And besides, I'm supposed to be there for her.

When the agent came out to the waiting area to greet the actor, she asked if Pammy had offered him coffee. "No, your receptionist did not offer me a goddamn thing." They both stared her into oblivion. I thought he liked me was all that went through Pammy's head. Her stomach fell into a spasm.

Later, she played it back in her brain but with a different ending. She's walking to the subway after work and a limo glides by and stops and the window opens, the tinted window opens and his voice, all gravel and sex, erupts: "Hey! Receptionist !" And they live happily ever after. Like those couples you see at the dentist's in People Magazine and you wonder why such a handsome actor was married to someone just like Pammy. Just like me. The happiest girl in the world. And then she had a neutral fantasy. And then the good. She banished the negative. The negative. Pammy knew it was always reality.

Please God, can I have this one, this new fantasy, so different? Can I have Cal?

On her way to Calvert's, Pammy had dropped several letters in a mailbox. That was the second batch. There would be more. It was fun, creative. It felt so incredibly constructive. It also felt like an old game but that was totally untrue. It only felt old because her mind had been there so many times. Always looking at the ads in the back of magazines for potential recipients. What would I have sent to that actor? If there had been time. If I had even had the chance. No matter. The fact was that Pammy had actually only followed through on this particular route once before— her boss at her last job as a receptionist. It was a small ten person advertising agency and he was the head of it all, the creative director, always racing in and out to meetings. In the door. Out the door. Walking right by me like I wasn't even there. But I see you. I see your little pony tail, your black jacket and t-shirt, your power walk. There was no formal mailroom in the small office. The mailman dropped everything on her desk by mid-morning and one of Pammy's responsibilities was to sort it all out. She was so excited the first day she noticed some Pammy-generated mail arriving for the director. Information on time shares in Puerto Rico. She had heard him talking by the elevator about never taking a vacation. I'm helping him. I will touch him and help him at the same time. She had found the Puerto Rico do-you-want-info ad in the back of Lady's Day and carefully cut it out. She filled in his name and the address of the X-Ray Advertising Agency. And then the info arrived and his secretary swooped it up and took it to his office. To him. He will read something I sent to him. He'll wonder how the time share people knew exactly what he needed. How it got sent. Who sent it. And maybe someday I'll tell him it was me and he'll be touched and surprised that I cared and he'll love me immediately and we'll live happily ever after.

But then one day, his secretary picked up the mail at Pammy's desk and started to complain about all the junk mail her boss was receiving. "I just toss it," she said. "He'd kill me if one bit of that crap ever landed on his desk." Crap? Crap. That means he's never read one, not one of them. Not even Puerto Rico.

Pammy quit her job the next day. But this time, this time with

Calvert will be different. There would be no intermediary. No secretary with postal power. Just me, the mail and Cal.

The door to Calvert's building opened and a woman with an ancient cocker spaniel in a shopping cart lumbered onto the steps. Pammy took a peek at her watch. Less than an hour till class. I guess he's not coming out. Then she saw Anton loping towards the building. He's awfully early. Why is he so early? Is he really going in? Yes, he is. He opened the door just like that. Maybe Cal is coaching him for something. Maybe Anton knows a neighbor of Cal's or something and is just going to visit before class. I have to pee. I really don't want to go back to that diner again. If I leave, I'll miss Cal. I just have a feeling. I just want to see him outdoors. In the sun. But the sun is setting.

George thought he'd get to class a few minutes early and finally ask Cal if he thought he had a future as an actor. He spotted her a block away. She was fairly camouflaged to the bark of the tree with her brown wool coat and brown plaid pleated skirt. He stopped and stared at her. She's totally casing Cal's door. What's up with that? She's watching. She's watching.

The sun set on them. Pammy at the tree facing the building door. George down the block, a frozen statue, gaze glued on her. I could be with her. Watching and fucking and watching.

They both spied Valerie striding towards the building. Purple coat with a large papier maché brooch. Scorching red scarf. Her home. Her man inside. Who are we to her?

It was almost time for class.

denial

I think nothing when I do this. No. This is not the truth. I think I am the musician. This is why I am, I know, very good at this I do. It is object, not part of anyone. I shut them out. I think only of what I am possible to do with my mouth, with my tongue. I think of me. The music. The sacred music. Do not talk because I do not listen. I am in my music and that is all. The secret sacred music. The teaching because I am the best of boys shining in my altar whites. The secret from father to son. I forget the days goodbye. The ugly. Only this, from the sadness and tears, what has saved me. Put a roof on my head in this city. Stop me from being losted. The payment for my dreams.

Valerie took the stairs. It was her new diet exercise routine. She was determined to be that girl again with the waist and the hip bones that turned her on when she felt them jutting out. She remembered when her belly was flat and smooth and her pussy so easily wet. I can be that girl again. That juicy girl.

She opened the loft door and let them quickly fall in and out of her peripheral vision. Registered the blond-haired boy. Registered Cal. She kept walking towards the back bedroom. Eyes straight.

Valerie: Oh, hello. So nice of you to visit us.

She shut the door behind her, suddenly short of breath.

Calvert: Brilliant.
He looks down, puts his hands on either side of Anton's head and pushes downward.
You too, my dear Anton.

Calvert is awash in the smile of his almost perfect world.

now class

They could all hear Cal and Valerie talking behind the door to the living quarters but their words were indecipherable. Sounds bouncing against wood.

George idly took his beeper out of his pocket and flipped it over and over and over. Seamus noticed. Anton. Pammy. Wissa and Chet. Chet whistled.

Man, you've got a beeper.
Yeah. I do.

George gave a big flourish of a flip to the beeper and missed the catch. It bounced onto the rug.

It's phone company issue. For really important employees.

He glanced at Pammy but couldn't gauge her reaction. The door opened and Calvert marched in from the back of the loft. All tech envy was forgotten. Cal surveyed his brood.

You have to take the bold move to advance your careers. You have to sell yourselves. Every day you have to find some way to market yourself. Do not be the fool who believes you will succeed with that great audition and ten notebooks of class notes propelling you. No. Arrive unannounced at an agent's office. Slip into an audition for which you have no appointment. Corner that casting agent in the bathroom of the restaurant where you bartend or waitress or bus dishes. The bold move makes the actor. Such a move may define you and possibly leave you breathless.

If they only knew, that I, their teacher on high, have never made a bold move in my life.

Maura's thinking: In what Dark Age did Cal do all these things? In any business, they just don't seem right to me. Aggressive can easily trip the line. Am I too meek? Will these kids do that? Or will the agents, the casting folk, whatever, just smell the steaming desperation and send them packing? Is he giving us bad advice? Is all his advice bad advice?

Calvert eyed each and every one of them. Pammy drowning in brown. George who had never seen an iron. Seamus with his strangulating bow tie. Wissa pale and transparent. Anton in dire need of a shopping excursion. Chet always in his starched white shirt. The breasts of Bibi aching to escape the ruffle of her polyester office shirt. And Maura forever cloaked in various inspirations of basic black.

Now that we have covered your outward moves, the bold moves, we move onto something more prosaic, but no less important to the forward movement of your, shall we say—

Cal shoots a glance to Bibi's bosom.

Shall we say, budding careers? What species of underwear are you wearing? You do not have to answer that. Looking at all of you, it does not take much imagination. What does take imagination and study are your wardrobe choices when it comes to an audition. A good actor dresses the character. Someday you will go into an audition for an outdoor hiker and everyone waiting will be wearing plaid flannel shirts. But what are they wearing for underwear? What if it were an audition for a cowboy in the 1800's? What then? In any period production worth its salt, the wardrobe designer takes great pains to recreate and put the actors in period undergarments. This is what makes you a whole person. A whole character. Complete.

Seamus thought of all the high school Shakespeare productions he had been in. What did Julius Caesar wear under his toga? Mark Antony? Mark Antony would definitely go commando. Commando Mark Antony. Of course. Totally appropriate. And Falstaff?

Pammy took notes. George was itchy and wanted to scratch his balls. Anton just wanted to get out of his briefs, sticky with cum. Because, yes, he had. He always did.

Calvert smiled. Each and every one of them will tuck this wee bit of underwear pseudo trivia away in the cabinet of supreme insider information. That is me: a font of supreme insider information. What dummies. It makes me laugh. His smile lingered.

Maura wondered why he was smiling. What goes through that man's mind? I really am beginning to think he's full of shit. She focused on the fat gold wedding ring on his left hand. A member of the club. He has no hair on his hands. None whatsoever. Gus had that black hair shadowing his fingers. That was sex.

Calvert continued: Obviously the theme of the day is what goes on below. Anton, please, that red box over there.

Anton fetches. George remembers when he was once the fetcher. But that was last year. Was it because he gagged? I was right to gag. He said so. He forgave me. He said it was because he was so spiritually formidable. Yeah, maybe spiritually but he sure ain't bigger than me.

Calvert rubs his hands over the box as if he were a magician. Painted in black on the side of the box: Miscellaneous Box. He lifts a large strap-on black dildo from within.

Oh, how did this get in here? This, my class, is a mistake.

Cal tosses it into corner of the room. The students giggle. That always puts them at ease. George remembers this bit. Cal tends to mostly forget George ever took the class before, ever heard him utter the very same words. Or, perhaps, he just doesn't care.

Now these are the tools of the hide-the-actor's-privates trade. Before we go through this imaginative collection, what do you think might be used on a set?
Wissa: Flesh colored underwear?
Chet: A jock strap?
Calvert: Yes. Sometimes also known as a dance thong to withstand the energetic leaping of male ballet dancers. Anything else?

Seamus: A body double?

Excellent suggestion. It will, however, be quite a while before any of you are high enough on the food chain of thespians for production to budget in a body double. Step up, please, Mr. Cohen. You shall be your own body double.

Cal pulls a thick fabric sock from the box.
A modesty pouch or, in the vernacular, a cock sock.
Seamus blanches.
No, my boy, just extend your hand.
Calvert slips the sock over two of Seamus's fingers.
This is exactly what it is. Note that I only used two of Seamus's fingers. I, of course, would need three.

George snickered on cue. Me. All five. All five ! Chet thanked Jesus that Calvert had not chosen him. Pammy remembered when she had stuck tennis balls in her bra just to feel what it would be like to walk around with major breasts. And then one of them had dropped out right on the sidewalk by the corner bodega. Bouncy bounce. The store cat had swatted it inside onetwothree. She never shopped there again no matter how quickly Mother demanded milk.

I can see your minds are wandering. Come back, class. Now they might use some tape or adhesive to make it stay on your skin despite what obvious friction might ensue. Glue, even. We all must suffer for art. To continue, Mr. Cohen, please remove your bowtie and unbutton your shirt.

The pale, flat, hairless chest was reluctantly revealed.

Calvert: Exactly the chest I anticipated for this lesson.

Seamus wanted to evaporate. Cal reached into the red box and pulled out what appeared to be a ratty toupé.

Now were this more expensive and better groomed, it might very well be a merkin. Merkins were mostly used by prostitutes in times past to vouch for their health. Various antidotes for venereal disease, like mercury, would cause a most distressing loss of pubic hair. Consequently, having a deliciously thick bush made you appear as healthy as a virgin. Like you, I suspect, Mr. Cohen, but of course, your bush would be red, would it not? Hair reinforcement is often needed, not just in the nether regions but elsewhere. So let us apply this to our friend's hair challenged chest. A little Top Stick, a very strong double-sided tape for wigs, and voilà!

Seamus stood almost motionless with the blob of hair plastered between his nipples. Please G-d, make this stop.

Bibi tasted the metallic tinge of blood. The inside of her mouth hurt from her teeth ripping. Her hands were numb underneath her thighs. Not to him. Don't do this to Seamus. He has the good soul, the sweet boy. And you, old man, you open that mouth and nothing but fangs. How can I stop him?

Cal reached once more into his treasure box and retrieved a packet.

For our female actors, covering your nipples can make all the difference, emotionally and visually. Here we go — self-sticking nipple protectors. They look like little flowers. Once they are on, you no longer feel truly naked. You will be as fearless and relaxed on the set as you are on the beach. Especially in bathing attire purchased from the racks at Bloomingdale's.

He winked at Pammy. Embarrassment. Exhilaration. Terror. She was an open target for every emotion. It left her exhausted.

Cal peeled off the backing and placed both nipple protectors on Seamus. One more dip into the box and Calvert was holding what appeared to be a sanitary napkin.

These come in various shapes, sizes, colors, thicknesses and they go below. Take off the safety-strip Mr. Cohen, put it on.

Seamus looked Calvert in the eye. All his internal engines remembered to finally stand up straight, respect the backbone. G-d won't make this stop. He made you responsible for your own life. Seamus pulled off the nipple protectors, the cock sock, the ratty chest wig, buttoned up his shirt and sat back down. I stop it. I. Not G-d.

Chet started to clap but hesitated when he realized he was solo. Calvert slowly placed all the items back in the red box of doom.

That, Mr. Seamus Cohen, was an excellent example of what not to do on a set. Never. I am the director. You do not say no. You do not resist.

Maura couldn't hold it in any longer.

Of course, you can say no.

Oh, I know you. You were some '60's bra burner. We're discussing pragmatism. Real life. To work, to be a working actor, you must follow direction.

Maura slowed her racing brain. How do you deal with someone like this?

Maura: Contracts. You said it yourself Calvert. You said every actor has a contract and you can write in it what you will or will not do.
Wissa chimed in: And there really are body doubles— lots of them, obviously for lots of people not just the big names. I see casting notices for them all the time in BroadLights. Someone else could've been Seamus. Well, if they'd wanted to.

You just do not get it. You are surely a group of potential, if not current, losers. I have had very successful students. I do not believe any of you will be considered one of them. I am ending the class early. Each one of you is to take a scene from that pile on the bookcase over there. Your names are on them. Be prepared for next week. Please move the chairs to the side. Maura, I would like a word with you.

Wissa poked Maura.

Some of us are going to The Shelf for a drink. Meet us?
Sure, thanks. Especially make sure Seamus goes. He needs it.

a hot mess

And off they go down down, clumping on the stairs. Cal changes the order of the chairs to calm himself down. Maura waits. And waits.

I'd like to leave, Cal.
Have a seat. That bench over there.

He pauses to give her the opportunity to watch him approach. He sits beside her. Is he going to refund my money? That would be a blessing from Mr. Blessing. Is he going to scold me for being a grown up?

My dear, you are an extremely handsome woman.

Not exactly the compliment every woman longs to hear. Where did he study pick-up lines? Next he'll be praising my sturdy legs. Perhaps he'll ask to examine my teeth like a horse. She knew what was coming.

They all know what is coming. They know I am about to ask them to share my bed. To absorb my wisdom directly through my flesh. Every sperm imbued with information.

Do I need one more married man? Especially one I'm currently paying to sort of somewhat teach me acting albeit in a decidedly strange niche, if that. The logic would follow that I pay him to teach. If I sleep with him – therefore I'm paying to sleep with him. Ah, it's come to that. And besides, after today. After how he took obvious glee in tormenting poor Seamus. Not never. Certainly not after that oh so casual display of cruelty.

Please don't take offense Cal, but I'd prefer to keep it a simple student-teacher relationship.
Simple? A gray area, at best. Your decision, though, shall be totally respected. I do, however, believe I will always regret not having experienced the joy of your caress.

Oh, God, spare me. The joy of my caress. Was that his Hail Mary pass? Now I know I'm saved. Bring out the violins. Maura smiled, escaped the proposition bench, raced down the stairs. Not often, but tonight a beer sounded really good.

It gave Calvert great pleasure to make his overtures knowing Valerie was in the back room. Cal walked over to his big Dell computer and searched for some porn. One strike. That is all it is. My world is an endless batting cage.

rocky redux

How many dark bars in new york city with music loud, the smell of beer varnished into the wood, waiting awaiting the crowds of young, anxious to spout, declaim, brag, invent themselves right on the spot — just how many are there? There's always one around every corner too rowdy for those over thirty or those with ordered lives or those with lives long eviscerated from drink stumbling into another night. But for the young— the darker, the louder, the better.

The Shelf was one of those bars. Half a block from Cal and Valerie's loft. Neither one of them had ever been there. But every student of Cal's had found their way there to commiserate at some point after a class. Tonight almost all of the current crop barreled in, with Maura late to join. They found a round table in the corner just vacated by six Jersey girls in for a spritzer before hitting the dance clubs. All sparkly and shrill, the girls eyed Anton as they passed.

Wissa was first to bring it up.

That was so not cool. He didn't have to do it that way. He could've just done a show and tell.

Yeah, it was a shame, Seamus. You was like pin the tail on the donkey. Get it? Dong-key.

George laughed at his own pun. It was the cleverest he'd ever felt. He didn't even know where that brilliance came from. Yes he did. He looked across the table and saw Pammy. He was brilliant for her. He was shining for her.

George, man, that's just crude.

Chet received a smile from Wissa for shutting down George. Maura let the thought that had been internally brewing go public:

I've lost track of the purpose of this class. His amusement or our education?

Anton countered with his usual enthusiasm but mostly none of them ever knew what was in his mind or what the fuck he was talking about.

All it is all important. Everything of the body. Everything before the camera.

Anton's loud voice caught the attention of two beer sogged twenty-some-odd-year-olds at a table nearby. One looked like a perfectly cast jock, a towhead with a menacing jaw. The other was short, Latin, broken-nosed. Their ears keened to words of sex, pornography, simulation and, most of all, acting. Ah, acting. It was stronger than any military radar. Some zooming sense of kinship mixed with competition. Go two feet in nyc and bump into an actor. I can see by your outfit that you are a cowboy. You can see by my outfit that I'm a cowboy too. You can see by our outfits that we are both cowboys. Get yourself an outfit and be a cowboy too. Something to that Kingston Trio Laredo effect was in the air. But something about the angry tinge of liquor added confrontation to the equation. The neighboring drunk guys stood up in tandem, actor erectus.

Hey, man. You guys go to that sex class? The one with the ads all over that paper BroadLights? I heard it was a scam.
Yeah, I heard only rank wannabees took that class. Kids from the sticks. A-holes going to nowhereland.

Broken Nose eyed Wissa.

Of course, if it was her I would go. We could do us some warm up exercises. How 'bout it, chickie? Method acting part of your routine? Yah hey !

Seamus stood up.

Yeah, bozos. Make noise but you don't know shit. And when you get on a set and don't know what a fucking merkin is and stand there like a jerk and can't find your light and play Hamlet in jockey shorts, they're going to laugh you back to whatever rock pile you crawled out of.

Towhead shoved Seamus.
Yeah right, little man.
Anton socked Towhead.
This is my friend.
And he be mine.

Broken Nose responded, slamming Anton.

George picked up his chair, but stood there frozen, a strange sculpture with no resolve. Chet slipped under the table. Pammy threw up on Wissa. Maura ran for the bartender.

A good time was had by all.

this isn't happening

Bibi had just gone through the turnstile at the subway when she realized her gray tote bag was not on her shoulder. Shit. I left it at class. The train was pulling in. I want to go home to sleep, to do a little puff of weed. But that bag had the brief she was supposed to finish re-writing for the next morning. If my boss had any sense of grammar, I'd never have to do half his job. Fifteen minutes of work and now look what it's going to turn into. Double shit.

Back. Back. Back. She rang the buzzer.

Yes?

Valerie on the intercom.

It's Bibi De Los Santos. I'm in Calvert's class. I left my bag behind.

She waited. Suddenly Cal's voice emerged from the intercom.

I found it Miss Bibi. I will bring it down.

This is the slowest fucking elevator I know. Why can't he take the stairs? I could be home by now. I could be—

The elevator door opened. Cal was wearing a blue velvet bathrobe accented with purple piping. A twenty-fifth wedding anniversary present from Valerie. Bibi had never seen anything so ridiculous. Boy, this guy got some skinny legs.

He held out the gray tote to her.

Thanks, Mr. Blessing. It's got my work stuff in it.
Very few people call me Mr. Blessing.

Bibi shrugged. So ingrained. Just looking at him took her back so many years. Men like him. You mind your manners, Dulce. That's a man. That's money.

Thanks for getting the bag. I have to go.

He grabbed her wrist.

No, please. Delay a moment. Perhaps leaving the bag was intentional? Subconsciously so. Or deliciously kismet?

What the fuck is he talking about? Get me home, please God.

Bibi. I would like to ask you to have an affair with me. I make no promises. How sweet would be the joy of your caress.

Did I hear him? She stared dully at Calvert. An emptiness consumed her belly. Her shoulders fell. Do I have a sign across my forehead? But Mami, there is no money here. But no, there might be something else. For someone else.

Only if you're leaving Seamus alone. For real.
What an interesting thought.

And Bibi raced out of the building.

Calvert popped a Cheshire grin. I am the most persistent of fellows. Yes, I am. He shut the gate on the elevator then leaned in close on it until his genitals barely touched the metal. He moved ever so slightly. Just enough to feel good. Why on earth would she bring up Seamus? Do not waste precious elevator time on that. I forgot how deliciously cool this gate feels.

What did I say? Why? Can I jump down these subway tracks? I be right back where the rats run. In the garbage. The stinking muck. No just doesn't come out my dumb mouth. How many years? But I made it clear, it's for Seamus. What is it in Seamus touches me? Well, that's the deal Mr. Blessing. Mister. God help me, please.

the origins of my name

Seamus left the bar feeling close to giddy. I clocked him. I was in a bar fight. Me. And I clocked him. Shit, that felt good. I feel pumped. I don't want to go home. I want to go out dancing. I want to have sex.

Hey, Jew boy. Spare change?

Her face was street ruddy, brown hair matted. She sat on the doorstep of a building next to a liquor store, an overflowing torn shopping bag crammed beside her.

Help a girl get a drink, why dontcha?
Seamus kept walking.
Hey, Jew boy!!

Do I really look that Jewish? He rarely thought of it. Bar Mitzvah days so far away. The womb of family less warm. They certainly had a weird sense of humor my hippie dippy parents barely one foot out of the shtetl. Both his parents were children of Holocaust survivors, their world view shaped by hope, guilt, dark humor, ethics and rebellion. So when it came to naming their red-haired newborn, their thoughts raced backwards and forwards and erupted in laughter. Dad's great-grandfather, Motl, had been the shammes for their shul in Sczuczyn – in truth, more a city than a shtetl. The shammes ran the show, knew everyone, knocked on doors to remind them to come to synagogue services. He was a big deal in family memory. Someone whose memory they thought it would be cool to honor. But since most every non-Jew in the states mispronounced shammes to the Irish long-A sound and since Mom had an endless life-long crush on long-dead Humphrey Bogart and was especially fond of The Big Sleep, they Irished up his name with hippie mescaline stoked whimsy. And so Seamus Cohen was born. The fighting Seamus Cohen. The know all Seamus Cohen.

Yeah, me. That Seamus Cohen. He remembered when he was eleven in Hebrew school studying for his Bar Mitzvah and the moment the Rabbi left the classroom, Pukhovitz and the rest of the bullies would push him into a corner and try to punch him, calling him an Irish dog.

And now this drunk. "Hey, Jew boy." Can you hear her Pukhovitz wherever the fuck you are? Well, this Jew boy Seamus proud to be Jewish Cohen just decked a guy. Just decked you. Yeah, you, fart face. You are so gone. Bye bye Pukhovitz bye bye.

Cleansed. Taller. Seamus headed downtown to go clubbing. To go clubbing. And maybe this time, I'll get inside.

from the rush of social to solo

Open open open. Maura struggled with the apartment key. Dove into the dark and straight to the bathroom, coat and scarf on, pants and undies down down down. How is that? How is it that you can hold it in from the bar to the subway to the walk home to the elevator and one second away from the toilet it's so unbearable you think you're going to wet your pants? No sweeter feeling than an empty bladder. Oh well, yes, there are others.

She put on the lights. Listened to the air in the empty apartment. Honey, I'm home. She put on some music and ambled back to her tiny galley kitchen. Maura opened the refrigerator door and stared inside as if some magic food might appear that she wasn't aware of. Like another human being had slipped in and left her dinner, a treat, a bit of love.

She was still feeling her beer, feeling the adrenalin of the bar fight, feeling a little horny too. From the cd player, Ella and Louis warmed the air singing "Our Love Is Here To Stay." Maura put one hand upon an imaginary shoulder and the other gracefully horizontal. She did an easy fox trot to the music. She swayed and turned and turned again. And if, perchance, you love to dance...

i'm on fire

George couldn't sleep for all the racing of his mind. So tiny. She's so tiny. And she saw me pick up that chair and threaten all those guys. Big George. Me. And she let me walk her to the C train. I know where she lives. I know where now. In Brooklyn. In a brownstone. That's so beautiful. That's so sweet. I wanted to kiss her but she smelled so bad of puke. Terrible bad. I bet she wanted to kiss me too, though. I ain't never been to Brooklyn but I could get there. And she would open the door. Pammy.

Brooklyn is a big place, George. Big old borough. Pammy in a haystack hot for me.

this life unbreathing

She opened the door as quietly as she could, hoping Mother was already asleep. But no, she was standing by the kitchen sink. Polishing silver. Great-grandmother's silver dead in a drawer.

Pammy, it's after eleven.
There was a sick passenger on the train ahead. We had to wait in the station till they gave the okay for the train to go.
Well, I worry, you know. And the tension. I get the tension in my head. My shoulders.

Pammy swallowed the image of Mother with her long grey hair unpinned and hanging loose on her shoulders. The beige flannel nightgown flowing out from under her liverwurst pink chenille bed jacket. She was standing straight and strong. Maybe she didn't expect me to open the door. Maybe I surprised her before she had time to run back to bed.

How was your typing class?
Okay.
Will you rub my shoulders, dear? And finish the polishing?

Mother, I have to use the bathroom first. It was a long trip.

Who is that girl in the mirror? My hair. My hair is everywhere. And no. What is that? She leaned in closer. There was a crust of vomit at the corner of her mouth. Oh, no. Everyone on the train saw me like that. She washed her face and brushed her teeth. Hard.

My typing class. My lie. I just don't want to share my dream, my adventure with her. It's a good lie, a smart lie. Easily covered because, in fact, I already taught myself to type at work. The slowest reception desk in the world. Prohibited from reading a book, a newspaper. But there it sat. That useless electric typewriter. I bought that book how-to and read it on the subway. Memorized each lesson, each chart, so I could practice each day. And now Mother thinks I'm going to typing school. She believes me. I'm lying. I'm acting. I'm lying. I'm acting. Mister G. Calvert Blessing, I am a very good actress. I have pulled the wool over my very sharp Mother's eyes. Take me. Take me.

Pammy, come out of the bathroom already. It's time to go to bed.

maura goes to work

Maura sat down at her drawing board. She liked coming in early to work. No elevator squeeze. Quiet. No phones ringing. No drama. She started to sketch a pattern that had been in her head since last night. Slivers of moon in a midnight sky. Silhouettes of birds seeking shelter for the night. There was no computer at her desk. There was one at the desk next to hers — Clark's.

He was a whiz at all that CAD stuff. She went over the acronym in her head. Computer assisted design. His ideas changed color in the blink of an eye. Blue sky. Grey sky. Green birds. Move the bird to the left. Rotate the bird ninety degrees. Tosses. Plaids. I labor. I draw. I watch my art unfold in hours not seconds, minutes. BAD. Brain assisted design. The neanderthal textile world of Maura Felix. The repeats assemble in my head. Fill my head. Leave all other thoughts behind. And Clark? He knocks those designs out in a blink and has time to chat with his boyfriends on the phone all day. Apples and oranges Maura. Clark's designs. My designs. Apples and oranges. The boss loves us both.

She sneezed. She sneezed again. She opened the old bruised leather purse to retrieve a tissue. There it was. What she had totally forgotten about from last night. Neatly folded. The scene she had picked up from Cal's class.

The page was titled, "Railroad Affair." Did this really exist or did he write it? Somehow, I don't think Cal is a writer. She read on:

The Conductor slid the bathroom door shut behind him. She stared at him, glassy-eyed.
She: That was the first time I've gone to the bar car.
Conductor: It did you good. You look even prettier with a little liquor on those lips.
He slid his hand behind her back and under her blouse.
Conductor: You've now become my favorite commuter.
She: Won't they miss you?
Conductor: We don't stop again until North White Plains. Twenty minutes.
She thinks.
She: Twenty minutes.
He undoes her bra from behind and pulls her towards him.
Conductor: Only eighteen left.
Their lips lock.

The office door opened. Clark waved good morning to Maura. She folded up the scene and stuffed it back into her purse. What crap. Who else picked this scene? Who am I playing against? Anton? George? Or maybe Cal likes to play all the boy parts. I bet he would.

I bet he thinks he's our conductor. Taking us on a journey to where? I should have taken some standard acting class instead of this, whatever it is. Not this claptrap. Not this claptrap from such an ego buffoon of a man. What redeeming qualities does he even have? I can think of none. Come on, you know him for two and a half hours a week. Maybe he grows fresh herbs for the poor or something equally and appropriately esoteric for a man like that. But there, in the class? Maybe he fulfills the needs of true exhibitionists who don't blanch when auditioning is contingent on nudity. This crowd? My wimpy classmates including me? I feel a whole lot of potential blanching there. And Cal, maybe he's the world's best bad actor. Every part of him certainly feels like a sham. The guy deserves an award for artificial artifice. Stop thinking about him. You could quit. You could quit anytime. You're paying per class. But I signed on for the semester. I've never quit anything. I never quit Gus.

Breathe, Maura. Be calm. What is it in Calvert that gets your goat? Besides everything.

What's the point? Could I even act passion? I have never faked anything in bed, especially not the proverbial orgasm. If I didn't feel it, I'd be silent and just work that much harder to make my lover come. My lover. To make Gus come even when my heart felt cold. To have it be finished so I could lie back with my own thoughts, in my own cocoon. But Gus, he could sleep, he would sleep with any girl. Each one offered some new surprise, he told me. A tasting menu of sex. When he told me that—when you, you bastard – told me that, you were inflated with pride. Mister honesty. Oh, that ego. How could you not know that every word was a knife in my belly? I don't care that you loved women. I wanted you to love me. And I've never been sure. Never truly believed. Always spending too much time looking for clues to convince myself of the positive. You steadfastly never uttered the words except that one time, like a dream. And you are long gone now, never to dissuade me from my doubts.

I know why I signed up for Cal's class. I know why I sleep around now. But real answers? What makes me alive and you dead? I can take my clothes off now without thinking. It's just a body. Barely the one I remember from years ago. But bare my heart? I believe my heart has grown numb.

The moon Maura drew was all sharp edges. Icy to the eye.

impetus

Calvert never wanted to leave the bed, the soft old sheets, the cloud of the comforter over him, the cradle of the down pillow holding his brilliant head. I am a body on display. I am deliciously warm. He could feel the cold air on his nose. Why leave the bed? The wood blinds were still closed. Cracks let the sun make polka dots on the brick wall. Sun. Warmth. There's food in the refrigerator. Water in the pipes. I never have to leave and face the masses, the peons, the ugly.

The phone ring disrupted his sweet peace. Cal glanced at the alarm clock on the night table. Two twenty-three in the afternoon. He sat up in bed to let his diaphragm settle. Always best to be in proper voice.

Hello?

It was Valerie on the phone. Oh, Valerie you break into my time alone. I forget you. It's my apartment. My loft. Go away.

Cal, do me a favor. I want to call the dentist about that double bill that came in over the weekend. The one they claim is past due.

Open up the checkbook and tell me when I wrote that last check to him and the number. Think it was the end of September but I need the exact date before I call.
Yes, Valerie.

She wrote the checks. She paid the bills. She made the investments. She made the decisions. She made the money. He found the checkbook on her orderly little writing desk.

You wrote it on September 22nd. It was check number 2310 in the amount of two hundred thirty-five dollars.
Thanks Cal. Gotta go. Have a meeting. Take care of this later. Bye.

Cal stared at the check register. The next check, number 2311, was in the amount of five thousand dollars and was made out to the ASPCA. He flipped through the pages. Check number 2342, five thousand dollars to The American Red Cross. Check number 2344, five thousand dollars to Fountain House. Five thousand to Planned Parenthood. Five thousand dollars here, there, everywhere. In October alone, she had donated sixty thousand dollars to charity.

He rummaged through Valerie's desk and found the folder with the brokerage statements. She had withdrawn one million dollars in November and transferred it to their checking account. That is our checking account. Our brokerage account. What are you up to? You are giving away my future, you—you.

Cal sat back down on the bed. He lay back and pulled the comforter tight up to his neck. He had a horrible weight in his chest.

A crushing emptiness. His head began to hurt directly above his right eye.

In that closet is my new tuxedo. Valerie took me shopping. Me, the man on her arm at that gala for the library. They were honoring her. I did not give it a second thought that night. Why were they honoring her? They honor major donors, you fool. Next, she will probably want her name on the wing of a hospital. No no no. Not my money.

I will not be left broke.

the bold move

On her way to Dolan's, Wissa saw a cube truck crammed with film equipment in front of one of the brownstones. She'd always noticed the building because of the pink stone teddy bear guarding the door. Two stocky guys were busy trying to fit sand bags into whatever space remained in the truck.

She mentioned it to bartender Billy.

Oh yeah. A big director lives there. Makes naughty movies. Not blue. Just naughty. He's Italian. Go ask him for a part. You're an actress, ain't ya?
A customer piped in: I can tell she's not that kind of girl.

I'm not that kind of girl. I'm not that kind of girl.

The customer, a regular, knew the neighborhood well.

I grew up here. My father was a haberdasher. And that director down the block, I know him and he was no more born in Italy than I was. Yeah, calls himself Falconi now and with the accent and the fancy tie. But it was Maxie Fulop when we was kids working out at the sokol — you know, the gymasium. Probably where he got the idea for the name. Yeah, probably. Sokol's falcon in Czech and that's what we was, Czech. All the kids in this neighborhood was. But when Fulop came out with that so-called soft core film in the sixties, they called it art 'cause he was suddenly an Italian named Falconi. Believe me, Maxie was making stag films before that. Blue. Very blue. 'Course you might think it's art but that's your generation, kid.

Billy took her aside.

Don't listen to him. Listen to me. I got your best interests. Even those kinda films need extras and they don't gotta be naked. I'm telling you not everybody takes their clothes off and you wanna know hows I know? My older cousin, Bonnie, she's almost fifty and she's been doing that for years. Never takes off a stitch but if theys got a party scene, they'll be giving her a call and she looks swell all dressed up and a paycheck to take home after. With you, your looks, piece of cake.

Dinner break at four. Instead of sitting in a booth with a bowl of watered-down New York clam chowder, Wissa races down the block to the brownstone. No headshot. No résumé. Where's the buzzer? Where's the doorbell? Oh, damn, this is not how I want to do it. She grabs the heavy brass knocker on the door. Bangs. Bangs again.

A pudgy, balding man answers. He has odd cantaloupe colored wisps of fried hair drifting over his forehead.

Is Mr. Falconi in?

Yes, he is. What do you want?
I want to ask him for a job. I work up the block at Dolan's.
Then you have a job.
I mean in a film.
You're an actress?
Yeah.
Can you clean?
Clean?
Clean. As in straighten up things.
I guess.
Mr. Falconi is currently not in production. He does, however, need someone to clean up his archives. His memorabilia. Would you do that to start?
I guess.
Come back this time tomorrow. Wear dungarees.

He slammed the door in her face.

Wear dungarees? Even my grandmother doesn't say dungarees. Well, Cal, that was my bold move. Let's see where it goes.

dreams

Dear Teenie,

You know I've been getting by doing some accounting like always. Shout out to Mr. Gorham my favorite math teacher (yours too and I think you had a big crush on him.) I didn't tell you this but last month I lost one of the restaurants I was doing the books for. They went out of business. It happens a lot in New York. Restaurants are a tough business. Anyhow one of the actors that I did taxes for last spring works in a hotel and told me I can make a lot more money there as a bell boy.

Chet stopped writing. He crossed out bell boy until it was totally unrecognizable. Instead he wrote "concierge."

Anyhow one of the actors that I did taxes for last spring works in a hotel and told me I can make a lot more money there as a concierge. That's the person tells all the visitors all the exciting things to see in New York and makes the reservations. Now I can hear you saying that's a step down from book work but I saw his numbers. I did his taxes and I saw and I know he didn't report half the tips he must have put in his pocket. It'll mean a whole lot more money for me. For Aunt Myrt and especially you. I'm going to get you that souped up wheelchair Teenie and maybe even a car with special gizmos. Maybe even you can drive a school bus again. Well, I got my interview with the hotel manager tomorrow and I got my toes crossed too.

You say a prayer for me, okay?

I'm going to sign off now. Got to sleep and look fresh for that interview. Fresh – that's me.

Your loving brother,

Chet

He folded up the paper and slipped it into an envelope. Bell boy to concierge was just a little lie. But he knew if he wrote bell boy Teenie would somehow see that as demeaning. She had standards. He went and rummaged in Aunt Myrt's kitchen drawer for a stamp. I hope she won't mind. Aunt Myrt. I'll pay her back for this stamp. He looked out the little window into the darkness of nothing an airshaft becomes at night. If I get that job, things'll be good. That guy said the hours would be okay for going on auditions. Not that I'm going on that many but you never know. But that hotel is so far downtown. I never even heard of Hudson Street and coming back late at night to Pleasant Avenue. I just hate seeing those big rats on the streets so late. Like cats. So big. But money in your pocket. It makes a man stand tall. Yes, it does. Hell, they probably got rats on Hudson Street too.

i can do that

If I do it, I could just show her. Like, hi Pammy, here's a little experimental film I just shot. A nature film. My nature film. My natural me. My docu-cockumentary. You just gotta smile when you hear that. I do.

George had asked around. Arnie, one of the tech guys at the phone company had gone to film school for a semester. This guy knows. He told me to head over to 11th Avenue to UCO. I thought it was a dumb name. Not much shine for film stuff. But Arnie, he explained even a lot of film freaks don't know what the acronym's for. Didn't want to let him know that I didn't know what an acronym was neither but he kept talking and it was easy to figure out. I'm no dummy. United Camera Operations. UCO. Yeah. Got it.

So I planned on going over and telling them I got a project that I want to shoot in slow motion. Arnie had told me you shoot it faster and when you play it at regular speed, it just seems slow but it's not.

Well I get to UCO and it seemed really small. The counter was four steps from the door but then I realized the back was pretty enormous. All these cameras on shelves. And guys working on machinist's benches. It seemed really cool. I wanted to be on the other side of the counter. I always want to be on the other side of the counter.

There were two guys there directly behind the counter: Checked Shirt and Bald Guy. I told them I want to shoot a midget throwing up in slow motion and what's the best camera I should rent for the job. And, you know, they didn't even blink an eye. Guess these film guys heard everything. But I'm not gonna tell them I really want to see my dick growing and exploding. Yeah, tell them that and I might get a blink. Yeah. So I ask their advice on how to shoot this barfing midget. Checked Shirt brings out this sweet camera. He says it's a Beaulieu 8mm and can shoot 48 frames.

Perfect for you, buddy.
Perfect for me. Great. So, tell me guys, any advice on how I should actually do this?

Hey, they're the pros, I'm thinking. Them I should listen to, not necessarily Arnie. Hey, he only did one semester. These guys must be in for life. And then Checked Shirt starts in giving me the skinny.

How tall's the midget?

Bald Guy pokes Checked Shirt.

Larry, they say little people now.
How tall?

I point to my crotch. They don't even suspect.

Well, you want to shoot from the side assuming your goal is the trajectory of the puke. Set the tripod low. Measure from the midget's mouth to the camera and—

My schlong to the camera. How do I stand still and reach out to make adjustments? Do I Scotch tape the measuring tape to a stick and hold it out to the camera? But who's to grab it? Maybe I can put a chair where my dick is and run back to the camera to turn the dials. Will they explain the dials to me? Shit. They probably think I'm a pro too. This is really way too complicated. I didn't think.

Hey, Mo. You still with us?

George shut down his brain and turned back to the two guys at the counter.

Yeah, I'm listening. Now how do I get it developed into a movie I can see?

Checked Shirt and Bald Guy exchange a glance. Did they roll their eyes? No. Don't go paranoid, George. They think I'm one of them. Bald Guy rips a piece of paper off a pad.

You mean processed? Give you a list.
Will they do — sensitive stuff?
Oh, is this a porno midget?
Little person, Larry.

George immediately had the same look as when his Mom found him nose deep in her underwear drawer.

No, this ain't porn. It's—it's art.

Checked Shirt snorted.

Yeah, we know art. Tell you what, Mo, go to 47th Street. Buy a camcorder. Have fun.

The wind hurt on 11th Avenue. It skated off the Hudson River, bounded into the hulking industrial buildings of the far west and slammed into puny mortals like George. Even with his head down, George felt his nose hairs freeze immediately. Head down. Beaten.

By the time he got back to his neighborhood, beaten had gone to anger to embarrassment and back to beaten. He stopped at the bodega to buy one Goldenberger's Peanut Chews, two Baby Ruths, a box of Chips Ahoy and some milk.

Look at that guy by the potato chips. Pants so tight I can see everything. I got a bigger dick than you, pal. And then George's shoulders slumped. Maybe that's all I am. And no one can see my big dick in these fat boy baggy pants. No one can see.

The cashier barely gave George's carbo collection a glance. He'd seen major grass-fueled feeding frenzies in his time. This was nothing.

That all?

No, I'll take this too.

And George reached for a bag of orange marshmallow circus peanuts. He looks around. Potato chip boy is gone. He probably had a date. Yeah, a date.

One more thing.

George points to the wall behind the counter.

Gimme a pack of those Trojans. The extra big ones.

confrontation whaddya know

Evenings are so much darker now with early winter sun anxious to disappear. Valerie hiked the stairs to the loft. Don't know if this is enough exercise to banish my disappearing waist. I think my mother had a waist until the very day she died. She definitely did. But my father's side. That's another story, a totally different set of genes determined to thwart any sylphlike aspirations I might ever have had. Big blond Kentucky women. Like me. I should be stoking a fire instead of crunching numbers. But that's Cal's job. I let him stoke the fire. Remind me I'm still a juicy girl. Well, not quite as juicy.

She unlocked the loft door. Cal was sitting in the big paisley chair. Just sitting. Arms folded like some peeved professor. I opened the door and I swear he snarled.

You asked me to look up the check for the dentist.
Yes, Cal. I took care of it. The receptionist—
And what about the checks for every charity under the sun? Large checks, Valerie. Not to mention stunning withdrawals from the brokerage house.

Valerie didn't quite know how to reply at first. Money was a subject rarely broached between them. Twenty-nine years of marriage, two years of dating before, and each had fallen into their own roles, their own tasks, their own secrets. And everything ran very smoothly. Well, it did.

What made you suddenly look through all that?
We are married. Not to mention, the dentist. You, Valerie, you asked me. It is our money, after all. Ours.
Oh, come on Cal. We're very comfortable. More than comfortable. We have no children to leave it to. Why not share? What's the purpose of hanging on to it?
There. Just hurling it away. That is the action you are so gleefully pursuing. This goes to the root of the problem, exactly. No discussion whatsoever and you have become a philanthropist.
Hardly.
More than I deem permissible.
Permissible?

It was a show down. It was rage and eyes glaring. Genders flaring.

Cal, you must be really slow. All these years, I've credited you with supreme intelligence. Why do you think we've been going to all those charity events? Sure, it's to network and find more clients – but I give and give. Why not? We can't bury ourselves with it. Cremate it. I'm taking a bath. Go sulk if you want. Or make some money for a change, Mister Bitterness. This is not what I want to come home to. Good God.

Cal got up and followed her into the living quarters. He stopped by the door. No words. No words. The rolodex dominated

Valerie's writing desk. Rolodex number two. Twin sister to number one in her office. A copy of every name, every phone number that fed into her income. Their income. She has her rolodex. What do I have?

He stared at his lonely work corner, his carved soap boats carefully assembled in a waterless harbor. Every business trip, she would bring home all the little hotel soaps for me to carve. Oh Cal, how I missed you as she handed him the soaps and shed her clothes. And one out of every five soaps was shaved and notched to morph into a small cameo of her. Now the days of her being on the road, the fledgling forays into finance, are gone. My soap inventory has become so low, I will soon have to purchase them. Buy them with my allowance from Valerie. Money, money, money. What do I have?

His eyes stopped at the pile of headshots in the milk crate.

I have fresh meat. And Valerie's rolodex. Oh, yes. Yes. That may very well be the combination to the safe.

if i was a

Anton filled half the cup with sugar. He tried to add milk but the coffee was close to the edge. My breakfast. My lunch. My dinner.

Someday I will be famous and this I will know when I see my headshot here in the Six Boys Diner. This is my diner and I see the headshots here. On the wall. So many. Some I know. Some look many years old. Have grease on them even. I see Telly Savalas. Him I know from the television in Poland. The detective. Never the dubbing any good. Mouth too fast too slow. Maybe I am shaving my head. Maybe there is no need if I be like Uncle Milek. No hair there. Oh and this picture there. That lady. I see her in a magazine one time advertising the prunes. She look some like Mama. With the round face and smile of kindness and sun. Oh, Mama. Be with me now. Be in my heart. I do not intend to do bad things. I want to be a good actor and famous. Famous Anton Grybowski. You will be proud.

This I will write on the headshot. Dear Six Boys. You have the best coffee. Respectfully, Anton. No. Maybe...... Your coffee make me famous. No. I love your coffee. That one.

Now coffee is all I can pay. When I give them headshot, I get eggs.

precipice the look behind

Bibi turned the corner. For this, I'm leaving work early? To go back in time? But her feet kept moving and she couldn't stop herself. Just like she couldn't stop herself when she saw Cal's ad in the open BroadLights Weekly left on the subway. It was the too familiar. The sewer reclaiming its child.

How many of his students do this guy have affairs with? Do he ask and ask and wow! Oh boy! I got one. Like some fisher guy at the river. Fish all day and finally he get some sick old East River fish. Catch a fishy in the new york sea. Looking sweet but poison to eat.

How long I been clean?

But no, Bibi, this time be different. I do this and he'll leave that Seamus alone. I set the rules. I can handle this but Seamus—I see Seamus grow small with all Cal's mean words. What kind of teacher got to be so mean? You lay off Seamus, Cal. That Cal's some kind of bully. But me, in that world, in that world of shove it in pull it out—me, I'm the strong one. Bibi De Los Santos. That's even funny in a sick way. But I won't tell Seamus this is for him. He wouldn't understand.

She rang the buzzer.

loop

Why does money consume my thoughts? Because it is not yours, you arse. It is not yours. The food you eat. The roof over your head. The toilet paper you gaze at to confirm the color of your shit. I am exhausted for want of her money. I do count the days now. I do count the days until that bloated mathematical bag of estrogen expires.

She will outlive me. It is an actuarial fact. I need my own sources. Resources. A call for a starring role. A major role for you G. Calvert. We tracked you down through your expired SAG card. The producer remembered you from that film you did in North Carolina. Oh, yes, that film. I was a young professor happy in tweeds. Deluded ingenue reveling in artificial adulation.

The buzzer rang on the loft intercom.

No calls for you, my dear Calvert. There is, of course, that other thought.

The buzzer rang again.

Please leave me alone. Oh, I quite forgot. It is my student. My special student. Cal rose from the double-pillowed chair, rose with a smile impossible to quell. All the wheels had turned simultaneously, riding into a sunshine of possibility. My students. My students. I know this is the perfect route to money. Do I dare?

He buzzed back on the intercom without inquiring who was in the street.

on the air mattress

Calvert stopped going down on Valerie after he witnessed just one more evidence of her penchant for penury. Penchant for penury. Every time he said it he felt he was channeling Shakespeare. Valerie La Cheap was sitting on the toilet, blew her nose with some wadded toilet paper and then used it to wipe her crotch. Imagine that. Wipe her crotch. He saw her do it once, then again and again. I am shaving and she has no shame. Anything to save a penny. It is a wonder we are not using corn husks. But that image. If I go down there, I am sure to find a booger in my mouth. No cunnilingus for you, Valerie.

But this Bibi. Oh, she tastes the lovely sweet sour I remember from my college days and with those dark Latin lady lips. I do like it.

Bibi glances down and sees the old man gray hair that is Cal. She feels the old man breath on her pussy and the gristle of his afternoon beard. Which one had white hair, gray hair? They was all a hundred years old. What am I doing back in time? She felt herself go dry. Knew the only moisture down there was his stinky spit. She pulled back.

Let me do you.

Let me make you come. Let me blow you, old man. And boom, it'll be over and I can go home, get under the covers, pile on the blankets till I can't be moving at all. Like a baby wrapped tight. Hold me blankets. Hold me like someone who don't exist. Neverwas. Neverwillbe.

She let her mouth relax and filled her head with religion. His penis was a disembodied object. Within a few moments of the blow job, she no longer noticed the sour smell of his body or maybe she had washed it away with her tongue. Her tongue prayed to his penis. She pretended she was a follower of some ancient phallic religion and this was her prayer.

Who teach me that? Who teach me clear your head, be in a pretty place? You have to ask, Bibi? She knew all the answers. Every hole of her body filled up every which way every day. And still she have time for me. Time to hold me when Papi Fannon wasn't looking. Mami, I'm hungry. She in the bedroom on her knees with a mister in her mouth. She wave me away, a smile just for me in her eyes. The mister, he blew me a kiss.

Clear your head. Be in a pretty place when the misters come and you all beautiful in your tutu. The misters could only go down there. That was the rules. Down with their cracked rough lips and slurpy mouths. Anything else, I'm supposed to scream to hell and Papi Fannon come running. Come running for more money and a one-two kick them down the stairs. But me, I always see the everything Mami do. And that's what I take with me that bad year in the street, on the wayback subway platforms, feeling dark and scared on my scabby knees. Fuck. I was still just a little girl.

Her mind left for another direction. How crazy that Cal wanted me to go into his bed. Be in that bed he share with his wife. Why'd that get me more upset than him? Maybe he gets off on that. Well, no way I'd get in your wife's bed, have to smell her smell on the sheets.

Then Bibi's mouth began to get tired. As good as she was, miracles were not on her résumé. Man, he go from hard to soft to hard to soft. Come already, old man. She glanced at the wall clock. Close to fifty minutes. No wonder my mouth hurts. She pulled back a little.

Calvert mumbled:
I'm on this medication for reflux. It makes it difficult to come.
He pushed her head down and whimpered:
Please.

Finally, he came. A little splutter which she swallowed not ever knowing what else to do. She never really saw what Mami done. And Cal he made this long long oh. Well, I accomplished something. I guess.

Has it been a while – since, you know – that happened?

Praise me. Praise me. Tell me that was the best blow job you ever had. I made this sacrifice. Give me some reward. Calvert sat up like a spring, totally startling her.
I am married, my dear.

With the emphasis on 'am.'

All the anger wells up inside her. Let your wife spend an hour on that old cock trying to get you to come. Bibi goes to the bathroom to clean up and stifle her rage. She looks around at all the girly things in the married bathroom. Bibi grabs the cup to rinse her mouth. She almost retches when she pulls a pubic hair out from between her teeth.

And it was old man's cum after all. Cum like cottage cheese curdled and it hadn't been aired in months. He's lying. Fuck him. Fuck him for making me be here. I made me be here. You, Bibi. It was you.

Bibi wrenched long black hairs out of her scalp and liberally strew them all around the bathroom. Find those, blond wifey. I was here. I was here. I'm not some invisible hole.I should be you. Never thinking twice. All the good things must've come slippy-slide your way. Ring on your finger. Money always in your pocket.

This was a mistake. Who am I thinking my whore ways gonna save Seamus? Well, they better, old man. You better never put shame on him again. Bibi opened the bathroom door.

Don't be forgetting our deal.
I forget nothing.
Calvert blew her a kiss.
Thank you, sweet Bibi. I do believe I might even love you with a small "L."

afterglow goes fishing

Love you with a small "L." How many times have I said that one? It forgives all the nothing that I feel and I do believe it warms their hungry hearts. Yes it does.

Cal yawned. I could take a nap or I could start my little project. My daring project. I feel this is a good time when I have some sense of power remaining in my loins. Rid of the nagging emasculation Valerie tends to emit. Here we go, Calvert. My project.

His challenge to that comfortable quicksand of passivity began. He spun open Valerie's rolodex and read through some of the names, seeking the familiar. Oh, yes. Monroe Vincene Cabell. Valerie had penciled in "heir to the Cabell foundry fortune — wife Lulu née Arjuk." Cal remembered Princess Arjuk. There had been a major brouhaha years ago at Studio 54 and she was at the center of it, bloodied but gorgeous nevertheless. Of course, he had only read about it and studied the photo splashed across the Daily News. And then, last year, Valerie had arranged a dinner for the four of them. The poor girl truly believes I am unaware that she exhibits me for various business reasons and hides me for others. Well, this will come to haunt you, dear Valerie. Your introductions will further my plans and gain me my freedom. Halleluyah.

Cal picked up the telephone and dialed Monroe's direct business number.

Hello, Monroe. This is G. Calvert Blessing. Valerie's husband.
Silence.
We dined together last year. La Grenouille.
Oh yes, yes. But how did you get this number? Only —
I must admit that I used Valerie's files. Monroe, I am trusting in your discretion. I felt an immediate kinship with you when we met and I would like to discuss a business proposition that you, and perhaps even Lulu, might well enjoy.
You've got my attention.
I know you have been a patron of the arts in the past. I remember, as well, that you found the hat check girl at the restaurant quite appealing. As did I. I am an observer and thus, I observed.
Where the hell are you going with this Blessing?

mr. falconi please

Wissa came back. Am I curious? Am I scared? Am I excited? Am I multiple choice all of the above? Well, I'm wearing blue jeans, the required dress code of the Falconi representative whoever he is.

She tackled the brownstone's heavy brass door knocker again. The little man opened the door.

Is Mr. Falconi in?
Why do you need to meet Mr. Falconi now? He gave you a job. Show him you can do it.
Are you Mr. Falconi?
Of course not. Do I look like Mr. Falconi?

Well that put the brakes on. Wissa didn't have a clue to his looks. I should have done some research. Relying on bar talk. Oh, you chowderhead. Wissa took a breath and decided to cut to the chase.

How much will I get paid?
You do the job, you get paid. Mr. Falconi is an honest man. He has a reputation. What do you have?

He leads her inside. Barely. In the corner of the foyer is a bucket with a broom, a rag and a dustpan inside it. The man gestures to Wissa to pick up the bucket. He opens a red painted wooden door in the narrow hallway. Steep stairs lead down to the basement. He flicks on a stair light but the basement remains dim.

Mr. Falconi has much valuable film memorabilia including many magazines. He wants you to sweep and dust. He wants you to arrange the magazines alphabetically by title and then pile them in chronological order. You may leave your coat on the bench here. When you finish, come back upstairs and you will be paid accordingly. When you reach the bottom of the stairs, there is a string hanging to turn on the light.

The little man walked away. Metal taps on his shoes clicked against the parquet floor.

Why don't I feel more scared? This is crazy. This is not exactly the career path to an acting job. Yeah, well you think waitressing is? Read a romance novel while you're at it. But it is crazy. He's the one giving me orders. Is he telepathically linked to this Falconi guy? He could lock me in this basement. I could be here forever. I could be one of those sex slaves you read about. Or he could see how hard I work and that I take direction well. Everyone says that being good at taking direction is the number one most important thing for an actress. Well, Cal said it. An actor. I'm not an actress; I'm an actor. Cal is always making a big deal about that distinction. That man in the bar did say this Falconi is really famous — well, sort of. I could be really famous. I'm young enough. I could still be an ingenue. That's how the really great women actresses started. Ingenues. Actors. Ingenues.

Down the stairs. The residual light from the first floor dims as she descends. Wissa sees the string for the light bulb and pulls, lighting up the basement. The small room was filled with stacks of magazines, glasses and loose boxes filled with matchbooks. What a fire hazard. Even with the bare light bulb on, the space was dark and dank. She could smell water or mold. She wasn't sure which. Maybe the East River is seeping up through the floor. Or sewage. Her hand passes through a sticky cobweb and she shakes it off.

On the floor, Wissa sees a tiny glass vase. Small and delicate. Frosted glass not more than four inches high. When she picks it up, it becomes apparent it's an old empty perfume bottle. Why is that here? Is this one of Falconi's collections? Or maybe he saved it from some famous actress. Yeah, famous porn actress. Or worse – the last idiot sweeping here decades ago had it in her purse, ready to dab behind each ear for the great director until they chained her to the wall and fed her to the wolves. Okay Wissa, stop the stories. Get to work.

She puts down the bucket. Grabs the broom. Starts to sweep. Something shifts in her peripheral vision. Wissa's legs freeze. It was the wall. The wall is moving. The wall is a solid sheet of water bugs. She drops the broom and slips the perfume bottle into her pocket without thinking. Bastards. The wall moved again.

She runs up the basement steps two at a time, grabs her jacket and races out the front door, slamming it behind her. The cold air felt clean on her face. Keep walking. Keep walking. About halfway down the block, she pulled the perfume bottle from her pocket and studied it. I know it's an antique. I just stole. I just walked off a job. I've never done either. Never.

Wissa marches up the street and right into Dolan's.

What are you doing here, kid? Your day off.
I want a Guinness, Billy. Please.
Sure. You got it.
He pats her hand.
But why don't you go clean up in the toilet while I'm pouring?

In the bathroom, the mirror confronts her. Cobwebs cling to her blond spikes like some old cafeteria lady's hairnet. She sticks her head under the faucet. What was that? I'm not that desperate for money. I'm not.

a commencement of missives

Not difficult. Pretty easy, in fact. Piece of cake. Piece of cake for a guy like me. I got the job, the smarts to make the connections, the smile "Hey gimme the password, Jimmy" and the bag of weed. Good work, George.

I should of been a detective. He knew she either took the C or the A. He picked up a recent subway map at the fare booth and checked out what neighborhoods in Brooklyn were on the route. I can do this. I can do this. Via his job at the telephone company, George finagled his way through company records instead of wading through all the Kemples in the Brooklyn phone book. Look at all these fucking Kemples. Who knew? And such a stupid name. With the phone company, he could cross reference neighborhoods and the subway line. All things those diggers had to be conscious of. Got to avoid those sparky explosions on company time. So there it was. In black and white. He was positively joyous God had planted all the other Kemples in neighborhoods distant from the A and the C line. Planted little spermy Kemples here there and everywhere but in Carroll Gardens right by the train. For that's where she was. The girl of his dreams.

The other four Kemple listings by the A and the C train were headed by male names. His listing, the one he hungered for, her listing, was under Margaret P. Kemple on DeGraw Street in Carroll Gardens. That had to be her mother. Didn't she say she had to go home to Mother once? That means Father doesn't exist. At least it means it to me. Margaret P. Kemple. Maybe even the P. was for Pammy or Pamela and maybe her mom named Pammy after herself. Yeah, some families do that. Spooky to me.

Address in hand, George began his mission. Touching air. He had accumulated a slew of magazines in preparation. He had rescued a good deal of them from his building's garbage. He wanted to have a wide area of interests to draw on.

He lied about having a dentist appointment to leave work early so he had time before class to get home. The moment he got in the door, he threw his coat on the floor and grabbed a bunch of magazines. The first ad George cut out was for traveling to Costa Rica. That's a good one. For the "Please Send Information To" line he carefully filled in Pammy's name and address. He put it in an envelope, addressed it to the travel company, licked a stamp and stuck it on. One down.

It was almost time to head off to class. He had completed seven envelopes addressed to schools, businesses, even government offices. One was for how to learn to draw, another was for franchising cookie companies. His favorite was for dog grooming school. He didn't really know but he had a feeling she really liked animals. And he thought she must be really kind because she was so quiet. I don't know that really goes together but

I think 'cause she don't open up a lot, she's got to have a lot of feeling. I got a lot of feeling. We'd be really good. Together. Together.

I still got time for one more. George headed over to another pile of magazines on the kitchen counter. Next to them was his industrial sized jug of French's Mustard. Coney Island size, pump and all. The back of the label caught his eye. A free cookbook of recipes using French's Mustard was offered. He quickly grabbed a piece of paper and wrote: Please send cookbook to, followed by Pammy's address. He copied the cookbook offer address onto another envelope and finished it off. Time to go.

The sidewalk was a minor rush hour of people coming home from work. George strode through them with purpose. All he saw was the mailbox on the corner. One by one, he slid the envelopes inside. Every part of him was functioning. Love letters in a bottle.

blow it up

Calvert looked at the clock. His little flock had begun to trickle in. Time to change the dynamic. He looked at Chet. Mr. Clean. Always in his sparkling white shirt. Who starches his collar? Never a speck of errant smegma on that lad, I would venture.

Mister Root, today you will blow up that air mattress in the corner. There is a pump beside it so no fear about stressing your fine lungs. Every week from now on, one of you will be in charge of awakening the mattress. Go on.

He relished the panic in their faces. This was their fear. Their want. For whatever reason, they wanted it. Badly. Apologies, children. I am a most exquisitely skilled tease.

Chet worried that he might be sweating. He stood up and loped toward the mattress. He kneeled down and glanced over at the group. Wissa gave him a quick thumbs up. I like Wissa. She's sweet.

Calvert observed the exchange. Mr. Clean and the cheerleader. Interesting.

scene study reimagined

Maura raised her hand. Those scenes we picked up last week —
were we supposed to have partners? You never mentioned.

Well, my dear, if you were not so very impatient, perhaps I shall
address the subject now. We are, however, still missing Anton.
Nevertheless, tell me, which scene did you choose?
I got the conductor and the passenger.
George: The trainer and the client.
Wissa: The teacher and the pupil.
Chet: The reporter and the interview subject.
Pammy: The ruler and the servant.
Seamus: The chef and the diner.

Bibi listens. Power. No power. Power. No power.

Bibi? Your scene?

I see his game. Why I'm playing it? Why I'm paying to play it?

The babysitter. The babysitter and the—
Bibi, we are all waiting with bated breath.

She stood up and grabbed her coat from the back of the chair. I can't do this. Just some old sick stuck in my head.

Actors are professional liars. I'm a paralegal.
Highly dramatic for not being an actor.
My lying days are behind me.

She shot Cal an angry eye. A searching glance at Seamus. He'll be okay. I fixed it. I fixed it. The class watched her in silence as she opened the door and almost got barreled down by Anton. Anton waved a supermarket tabloid, Star Scoop, filched from the clinic.

I read this magazine and this she-devil comic says the grunting extra on top of her is no actor.
Calvert: That should have been worth an upgrade to principal, I would think.

Anton is not ready to give up his platform.

I read this and this is what she says. She says extra is no actor. No actor? I am an actor and so are the others. We do plays for no money and films for the students to grow and explore our craft and help them be Martin Scorcese someday to come.

Calvert's brain is just tickled. Ah yes, craft. My craft, my voice, my instrument. All those hideous actor words. Even my Pole is marinated in the vocabulary.

Anton marches to the center of the room, dwarfing Cal.

If there was no extra in the back, there is being no front. I do everything to be an actor and explore everything. I do this.

The class clapped in unison. Bibi was gone from their minds entirely. Left the room. Not a moment for them even to ponder. Except for Seamus. His clap was so weak as to be silent. What really set her off? Where did she go?

I do everything to support my family. To send them money.

Cal is surprised by Anton's admission. I did not expect this one to have a family. More like an independent amoeba sent to awaken my flaccid penis.

Anton hurled the copy of Star Scoop to the floor.

I no more laugh at her jokes on the television in the bars this comic. What is to make her an actor? I spit on her — ptooie.
Wissa: Ugh. Anton, did you just spit?
I act spit. I am an actor.

devolving

Now, individual performances aside, we have a class agenda to fulfill. I will assume that each of you read your scenes despite the fact that there was no scene partner at hand. True? Your actual homework was to envision it, to become both of the characters. Highlighting your lines and disregarding the person behind opposing lines defines stupidity. You must let the script envelop you and advance your imagination. Perhaps the situations led you to thoughts possibly frightening, possibly titillating. Did any of you go there? Did any of you find the situations arousing?

Most everyone found sudden fascination in their footwear.

Very well. Let us take a different tack. Are you capable of writing your own scenes now that you have been led to water?

The silence of no replies infuriated Calvert. His knee-jerk reaction was to seek a target. His preferred target. What was it that Bibi asked of me? Could she possibly have a crush on him? No matter. She is gone from the room.

You there, Red.
Seamus.
Red. Seamus. You do not talk enough.
I talk.
Enough was the operative word. Shy? Or perhaps you feel—
Calvert paused for dramatic emphasis.
Perhaps you feel torn, just being here. Tell me, son, are you gay?
Seamus examined his hands then looked hard at Cal.
Yes, I am.
Well how DID I know?

Fuck you, you old homophobic asshole. Those words stayed in Seamus's head but beamed hot arrows from his blue eyes. To avoid contamination and possible attack, Anton counted loose threads in the worn Persian rug. I make myself to be invisible. Cal's eyes swept around the room. No one made contact. He continued playing the teacher. His own spiteful version of the profession.

Personally, I am very thrilled that Mister Cohen is with us. I do not say that with any sarcasm. He represents a great tradition in acting. The heartthrob with a hard-on for the boys. Rock Hudson. Monty Clift.

Cal was always sure to say Monty, not Montgomery, as if they were friends. As if.

Wissa interrupted: That's supposed to make him talk more?
No. That is supposed to make Mister Seamus Cohen rise from his chair and take Mousey here into his arms and act.

Seamus stood up, still glaring. Pammy ran to the bathroom. Her voice cracked through the door.

I'm not ready. I'm not ready.

Calvert smirked at Seamus.

See how powerful a little testosterone can be?

and my thoughts take me home

Seamus hit the stairs running. I want them all behind me. No after class chit chat. No—sympathy, empathy. Poor Seamus. No poor Seamus me.

Did I come here to be humiliated? Did I envision myself paying to hump someone? Isn't that what I do already? This class is a joke. No wonder it was so cheap. Cal is an idiot. I think he's some closeted idiot. If I ever got a part, I would do what I do in real life. Pretend. Pretend to be happy. Pretend to be focused. Pretend to have goals. I don't want to see any of them again. Maybe Bibi. I like Bibi. I think she likes me. I think she's lonely. I don't have to be straight to like her, to want to hold her, to have her hold me. I want to hold her because she's warm and lonely and I'm lonely. And it's a comfort. Nope. No comfort for me. Once a stranger held me afterwards. That was nice. That was years ago. But it could happen again. Anything is possible. It could happen again.

I'll call Bibi tomorrow. We both left that class feeling pretty awful. I know. I know we have something to talk about. Lots to talk about. I'll call her tonight. No. Not tonight.

Tonight, I need a drink. I want a drink.

Twenty minutes later, he opened the heavy wooden door to The Sweet William, a bar he liked to go to in Murray Hill. It was a quiet bar, low key with white stucco on the outside and a small dark grey oval awning that felt very 1930's to him. Definitely not a dancing bar. An eying bar. A conversation bar. Just right, said Goldilocks Cohen. Seamus would sit at the bar. If he needed a conversation starter he always had his celebrity crush ready to go. The perfect conversation starter: Tom Cruise. Bring on the boxer shorts. Bring on the scientology rants. Just don't walk away. But they did. Conversations were brief. A word on his right. A word on his left. Seamus rarely met someone to remember his name. But he stayed long into the night. Early on, he learned to avoid beer or mixed drinks or soda. Those liquids went down too easily and he ended up spending more money than he could afford. He started ordering bourbon. Maker's Mark, straight up. He didn't really enjoy the taste but that made it all the easier to nurse. That one drink could last the entire evening. Much more economical.

When he did try to flirt, it was usually with the bartender. Sometimes he left him a ridiculous tip which totally eliminated his bourbon savings. He knew the bartender lived upstairs. Seamus had overheard a conversation about it. The bartender's name was Francis and he had a deep scar on his left cheek from his infantry days in Vietnam. The scar turned into a "z" when he smiled and some of the regulars even called him "z." Seamus loved the rivulets of wrinkles around his eyes and his broad shoulders and the fact that everyone in the bar obviously wanted to sleep with him. And some did. That's how Seamus knew about the apartment upstairs.

But tonight Seamus was determined. It was almost closing time and the crowd had thinned out. He glanced at the bartender's hard profile. Even the bourbon could not quell the adrenaline from Cal's class. Tonight, I just want. I want.

Francis ambled over to his end of the bar and smiled.

Did he read my mind? Is that maturity? Seamus returned the smile. Francis pulled a lone key from his jeans pocket and put it in Seamus's hand.

Wait for me upstairs. 2C.

Seamus fumbled for his wallet to pay his tab.

Forget it, kid. Go.

Seamus left the bar without a glance backwards. He felt his heart might shoot through his brain. The cold air was a quick stroke to his face as he pivoted into the little vestibule next door. He panicked that he didn't have the key to the main entry door but then noticed it was ajar. I guess Francis knew. Maybe he always makes sure it's unlocked for closing time. Erase that thought, Seamus. Now. He went up the stairs two at a time. He made a right and saw a door marked 2D. Seamus turned and found his destination, 2C.

He unlocked the door and was surprised to find a tiny studio, almost empty, messy. There was a double bed and a lone chair piled with clothes. Seamus sat awkwardly on the bed. He practiced sitting in different positions, trying to appear more casual.

He waited. A half hour went by. Forty-five minutes. Closing time had come and gone. Did he forget me? Does it take a really long time to clean up the bar? Did he maybe go back to someone else's place? Seamus waited another twenty minutes. There was no more adrenaline good or bad. He left the key on the bed and went home.

the sex issue

Climbing up the subway steps, Maura wondered if any of them were there to act. What a strange, impulsive move I've made. Not the first. I just feel so invisible lately. I want to remember what visible felt like. When heads turned. No heads turn now. No whistles or that awful gooey slurping sound men make with their lips. None of that.

She remembered when it happened to her mother. Only years later did the incident make any sense. Maura was sixteen and awkward with the attention her body was gathering. Mom and I were going to the beauty parlor, wasn't it? No the seamstress. She was going to take in my party dress because my waist was so small. Twenty-two inches. What I wouldn't give for a waist like that now. And we passed a construction site and the workers whistled. And my beautiful mother, the classic bombshell blond, said so quietly I wasn't sure she was talking to me — she said, "They didn't even look at me. They were looking at you."

At the time, the comment upset me. I didn't want those workers looking at me. Protect me with your beautiful body, your beautiful face, your beautiful hair, Mom. But no, not to happen. That was her moment. Her moment when she realized she had become invisible at age forty-three.

And now. Me too. Invisible women. God help the first asshole who calls me Ma'am.

Maura stopped at the newsstand. I won't be invisible. Not yet. She saw the magazine she had been noticing all week. The magazine that told you where to go, what to do, how to drown in the culture of the city. Or the underside. And this was the week. The special edition sex issue. I am the outsider. Let me back in. Let me in.

welcome mat

Seamus opened the door to his apartment and the tears defied his desire for them to stop. Guess no one's holding me tonight.

He let the hot water run to scalding and soaked a washcloth in the sink. Like a barber he swathed his face and let the steam calm him. Over and over. And later, as he lay in bed, he was lost in mind circles. Brain off. Brain on. Is it that I can't connect or I don't know who I want to connect to? A sherd of moonlight brightened one wall. Is there even a howl within me? The howl that says I'm here.

Dawn and Seamus was back out in the street. His feet led him to exactly where he wanted to go. He'd passed it going to every class. The small sign beckoned to him: Morning minyan 7:30. The tiny one story brick synagogue was wedged between two office buildings and had been built, so said a bronze plaque, in 1908 for the glove workers who once labored nearby. Do they make the minyan nowadays, he had wondered. Or do they open the doors in a panic, hoping to rope in the tenth Jewish man? The prayers that require ten. The actions that require ten.

You can pray alone in your room. You can pray alone in the dirt of your brain. You can pray alone with the cock of a stranger jammed in your mouth. But some prayers require community. Some prayers require the tribe. And it's Thursday. Time to read the Torah. If I go backwards, do I go forward? The sun was barely rising. He could see the eastern light dancing toward him in the street.

It was 7:15 and the wooden door was unlocked. Seamus touched his fingers to the mezuzah and entered. He saw yarmulkes and tallesim piled on a shelf. He reached out to take one and a rough Bronx voice stopped him.

You Jewish?

She was a short woman, round and squat with swollen ankles. Her hair was dyed jet black, so out of place with the age of her face.

You Jewish?

Is it my red hair? Lots of Jews have red hair. Even blond hair complete with blue eyes. Thank you slaughtering, raping sperm spewing Crusaders invading our Semitic dna. But he kept those words inside, crowded close to the insecurity, the random anger. Instead, he spoke with new calm. A calm that matched the sure steps that led him through the door.

I'm a Kohen.
Wonderful, wonderful. I'm Sadie. You'll have the first aliyah. You can read Hebrew, right?

He nodded yes.

You know, I used to be a redhead too. Back then, God knows how many years, you could see me a mile away. They'd call for the bucket brigade, I was that hot. Hah! I was, I tell you. So, are you saying Kaddish for someone?

Seamus let his thoughts speed. Who am I mourning? Who do I say goodbye to now? Can I lose the anger? I'm better than everything I've done that I don't want to remember. I'm better than that class. People will know Seamus Cohen for something wonderful.

Honey, you okay?
Seamus grinned. Sadie smiled back, two side teeth missing.
You put your tallis on now, honey.

She turned away to greet a stooped, wispy-haired man and stage whisper:
He's a Kohen. Just walked right in from the street. Gott tsu danken.

Sadie waved for Seamus to enter the sanctuary. He knew he would see this wrinkle of a woman again and again. He was home. For now.

digesting times three

When he was in the neighborhood, George liked to eat lunch on the median. There were benches on the medians on upper Broadway and he'd sit and watch the people cross the street. Cross right in front of him. Every kind of people. Just walking right by. No better show in the world.

He unwrapped his hero and toothed a big bite. A sliver of provolone fell on his jeans and he flicked it off. A nearby pigeon took note.

George saw the mailbox on the opposite corner. When will they touch base? When will all those how-to's, school guides, recipes, all the fill-in-the-address-to-achieve-your-dream-ads reach sweet Pammy's door? God, I hope the address is right. This isn't the best of me but it's me. It's me taking the reins. Making the move. At least I always got a plan. Or sort of.

First tentatively, then with obvious perpetually ravenous intentions, the pigeon began pecking at the cheese. George got up and left the half-eaten hero on the bench. Some hungry joe can have it or this ugly pigeon here. I gotta buy some more magazines.

you in this room

She never played music. She listened to the steam or the clank of the radiator pipes. Horn honks, planes, sirens. Let them be safe those firemen. Let them be safe. Sometimes children. Why they be out so late? Take them home. Wrap them up. Let them be safe. Let them be safe. Sometimes all she could hear was the sound of her ears. The vaguely high pitched metallic sound that could so easily surround her.

The intercom erupted into the room. Every cell of her changed. Who? She looked at the clock. Ten to eight. Who's coming to see me at night? Who comes to see me in the day? My place. My own and I don't want no one, anyone not ever inside.

Again, the intercom.

I don't have to be here. They could be buzzing to get into the building. Just random buzzing. Just buzzing looking for some dumbass. Well, I ain't no dumbass.

Intercom buzz.

Bibi couldn't help herself. Just hearing a voice wouldn't, couldn't make her hit that button, unlock the door. Just who is it? Just, "who is it?" That's all I gotta say.

Who is it?
It is Calvert, darling.

She had no thoughts. She had all thoughts. He's here? All the way here. She could feel her insides hiding. All the way here. My address. No, he's got it on the records. But this is my address. My address. He belongs in his. It's eight o'clock. Night. And the buzz so loud. So loud. He be buzzing again and again.

I know you there, Cal. It's late.
Are you alone?
Yeah, I'm alone.
Then?

She looked around the studio. Everything was a mirror of deliberate tidy. Just like her. He won't find dust. He didn't say why he was here. Maybe it's about school or he needs my help. Bibi, you know what he needs.

Buzz. Buzz. Buzz.

She buzzed him back.

in a spin

His brain was crowded with thoughts. Wow, the last twenty-four hours. The class, Francis standing me up, the synagogue. He took a toke of a joint and poured macaroni into the pot of boiling water on the stove. He stared at the pasta plumping up. Seamus special du jour. Add a little ketchup. A little oregano.

I went into that bar with my Tom Cruise starter conversation, my practiced Tom Cruise lust. I throw him out. Enough with the white boxer shorts. What scientologist peon is designated to bleach them bright white? I want shorts stained and soft from hundreds of washings. I know who must have stains like a real person. Like a human being. Like a mensch.

He threw out his dated Tom Cruise thoughts and went back to his secret crush, the yiddishe comedian Y.P.L. He never voiced his name. Such a secret. You were supposed to like the cute boys, the muscle boys, the body boys perfectus erectus. But within, it was the nasal voice that claimed him, the knife slash wit, the face imperfect, acne scarred. Tom Cruise? Be honest, Seamus me boy. My equivalent of a blond shiksa. An uncircumcised scientologist. My grandmother would plotz.

Secret crush. So secret I wouldn't even let myself indulge in it. Push away that thought. Be with the in crowd. Let me in. All my fantasies are correct. But when I did let myself, the time was sweet and alone and in the comfort nerve deep in my brain. Of course I know Y.P.L. is straight. What does that matter? It's my fantasy and he suddenly realizes he wants me. I'm glad he's Jewish. I'm glad he's circumcised. That counts. That counts with me.

Seamus remembered that pick up on Fire Island complaining after it was over that one of Seamus's red hairs was caught in his foreskin. Seamus thought he was going to puke right then and there.

He saw Y.P.L. last summer walking down Columbus Avenue by seventy-third street and he was with a beautiful henna-haired girl who was chattering away in Italian and he was nodding. Real serious. I guess he speaks Italian. Or fakes it. Maybe he just talks in English with an Italian accent and they all understand him perfectly. That would be just about right. She was wearing some flimsy, white cotton Indian shirt with white embroidery and Seamus could see her bare breasts right through it. He could see her breasts right there on Columbus Avenue. And so could Y.P.L. Did it make Y.P.L. hard? It made Seamus hard to watch, to think of the two of them oozing sex right there on Columbus Avenue.

I am always a better man without a man. I am always a better man without the drama of a relationship. Relationship? Four days here. Three days there. A brief boyfriend versus a one-night stand. And those don't count. I will them away. Oh, yeah, I was in a relationship with so-and-so. That's my story. Emptiest four days ever. That's my reality. What does it matter? I'll never see any of them again. No contradictions at my table.

I am always a better man without a man. I am a better man in fantasy love with Y.P.L. who lives in a different world, who may not even exist as the person I see him, who has no consciousness whatsoever that I dream of him. We talk in my head and pass looks and understandings. Am I fooling myself? Is this enough? Is this all I'm worth? Know your place, Seamus. Know your place which is no place.

No. I spit that thought out. I refuse to stay there. I'm not there now. I refuse to go backwards. I refuse. I refuse. My body shakes with refusal. I'll tell myself a different story. There is a yes. A yes molto grande. A nice Jewish boy with my name on his yarmulke. And maybe next time I go back to that synagogue, there will be Sadie standing there with Y.P.L. I'd like you to meet my nephew, she says. Her nephew. And me.

tutu

Bibi came out of the bathroom to find him sitting on the bed.

No. You can't be there.
So sorry, my darling. Shy of beds. So unique. I assumed it was just mine. Well, then, the couch? The floor? Or, perhaps, the road?

The empty look tells him The Beatles are not in her repertoire.

How did he get in here? I thought I'll come out the bathroom and he be gone. His water sky eyes with no lashes. His farty breath. It was a one time thing for the kid. Yeah, you tell yourself that, Bibi.

Cal walks toward her. Arms out like a Madonna.
My darling. Ah, my sweet. My sweet.

Mi dulce. Mi dulce. Dulce. Dulce was all she heard.

I could be your daughter.
Is that what you are shy about? Sex should have no boundaries. No boundaries. Why else would I be here? And with you.

Her beautiful mouth disappeared into a thin meager line.

And, as I assured you before, my sperm are quite dead so you need not fear another generation will arise. Here I stand, my darling, soon to be naked, my heart open before you. I do believe I could even love you in this little room. Yes, in this little room. Away from everyone. Not a witness in sight to my desire. Oh, sweet Bibi, I ache for you.

What play did I steal those lines from? Or am I finally waxing poetic in my older age?

I need you to make me come. I dream of it.
Every word sliced into her ears.
You are so skilled. I dare not say these words, but— Ah, my sweet, you must take it as a compliment. You are a true professional in the art of touch. It is a compliment. It is.

His florid words lost their timbre as he tried to whitewash the insult escaped. His actor voice left the room. Something in her eyes frightened him.

That was one time. One time for you to leave Seamus alone. Remember?
Oh, yes, Seamus. I do not think about him. I think about you.

Bibi, you stupid, stupid girl. I did the knee jerk sex thinking it was worth the money men spend. Thinking it might have some weight with Cal like all the justice scales they got all over my office. Cal never heard. Cal never really heard me say nothing. His ears were full of pussy.

She walked towards him but they didn't meet. Her fists were clenched stiff. Her arms rigid. All her words were lost in the acid of anger scorching her throat.

Cal backed up. He backed up until he was leaning against an assembly line bookcase neatly exploding with books. She reads. Oh, the child reads. Maybe I could bring up literature to calm her down. Calm is certainly not her current adjective. Everything about her face was a threat. Cal felt a dampness hot cold in his armpits, his back. Could she hurt me?

Bibi's mouth opened wide but no words emerged. A ragged exhale. She tried again. This time a NO sprang out that easily tipped the decibel range into hearing loss. Cal felt the sound deep in his chest. He went concave. Later, he would swear to himself that he heard car alarms go off.

No.

Like some ancient linen cloth unearthed in a careless excavation, the tutu evaporated into dust.

public space

Not much of a day, but he had installed a phone in an east side apartment. The lady was maybe forty, maybe even fifty, and George thought she kept looking at him. Well, either she thinks I'm going to steal her baseboards or she's got an eye for my ass. He crouched to secure the modular jack to the wall knowing full well the crack of his buttocks was exposed. Look at me. Look at me. He felt himself get aroused. Hey, she lives alone. I can tell. When was the last time she got any?

George waited for the subway. Five o'clock rush and all the long legs, the coats and scarves and breasts crowded about. Guess that lady wasn't in the mood to get any today. He'd never make a move. Not that I'd make my move. I got my career to think of. But if she'd of touched me, let me know, I would've done it. I would've known what to do.

Exactly what to do. 'Cause how many years, I been thinking in my brain what everybody's been doing? Thinking how my neighbors be doing it. Those kids in class. Even Cal and his big wife with her big boobs. Sometimes George is right in the room with them or watching from a roof and they wave to him and invite him to join the party. Yeah, I'd know what to do. And Pammy. His mind went blank.

The go home train was tight and overheated after the cold on the platform. George pushed to the empty middle of the car. Why does everybody gotta crowd the door? Why do they make it so hot in here? He found a space in the middle and grabbed the rod just as the train jerked to move. Sitting in front of him was a woman with her coat unzipped. George stared down at the cleavage of her breasts. He looked around and saw exposed skin popping up everywhere. Why are these women always doing this to me? He looks back at the woman in front of him, her eyes glued to a magazine, oblivious. Her cleavage was parallel to George's crotch. My cock. Her breasts. I could just reach down and unzip my fly. I could pull it out and she would—oh my God, what would she do?

Suddenly, he was furious. She'd get me arrested. She'd fuck up my entire future life. The thought invaded into his reality for the very first time. My future with her. My Pammy. The anger hurt it was so explosive. The train came to a stop and the woman stood up face to face with George. She felt the set of his face and it chilled her. She shoved her way out of the car.

George thought for a minute of following her, getting her address and mucking up her telephone line from the street. He'd done it before. He had his telephone i.d. He had that power. But not today. Today he slowly defused. If I'm gonna follow anybody, it'd be Pammy and I wouldn't do nothing to her. I'd just follow. I'd follow even though she ain't got no boobs. I do follow her. I send her my soul.

the ordinary of humdrum

Valerie came in from the street and opened the mailbox. She had left the office reluctantly. So much to do this early time of the year. She was the New Year's resolution of every client and every potential client. Make money. Squirrel money away for the inevitable rainy day. She had learned, with the soothing aid of too many self-help books, to make time for herself, her passions, amidst the whirl of work. And these events, these charity galas, were her joy. Her pride. The glow just spread through every layer of fatty cells that encircled her heart.

This is the second day that Cal has gotten a ridiculous amount of mail. I'm beginning to lose sight of the expanse of his craziness. She opened the envelopes one by one. Junk, junk and more junk. He seems to be mailing away for information on everything under the sun. Sponge monkeys. Body building. Look at this one. Turn Your Bathroom Into A Profitable Greenhouse. The man is mad.

And possibly dangerous. I knew he was upset about the donations but I never dreamed. God, let that whistle blowing be for nought. But still, I had to act. I had to.

Valerie threw all Cal's mail into the hallway garbage can before heading up to the loft.

set in motion

The tux felt a bit snug. Well, if we continue to go to all these charity kiss me on the cheek old boy fart galas, I will just continue to devour hors d'oeuves and Valerie, my bride, will be obliged to fork up funds to buy me a new one to further her philanthropical career.

Valerie put on a gown of maroon silk charmeuse with panels of deep purple to slim her down. A loose matching jacket softened the swell of her arms and hid the lumpiness of her waist and hips.

Cal? Please?

And then she asks me to do the clasp of that atrocious sundial thing around her neck. The woman is a walking weapon with her taste in jewelry. Moneymoneymoney. I have no need to ask what that monstrosity cost. I can feel it cutting into my waning years.

Cal leaned in to secure the clasp. In spite of himself, the smell of her warmed him. Made him feel safe and loved. He remembered the one piece of jewelry he had purchased for her. The engagement ring. From Macy's. The tiniest chip of a diamond.

Barely a hint of a diamond but jazzed up with a little surround of marcasite to give it some class. And Valerie, my Valerie, was thrilled. Not so sure about her parents.

Do not be ridiculous, Calvert. You are perfectly sure. Even now he cringed at the memory of their tight faces every time they met. As if his insertion into their family spelled doom. He called them Mr. and Mrs. until the day they died.

Seven weeks before the wedding they were incinerated in a crash on the Cross Island Parkway. Fog. Rain. A truck above the height restrictions. An overpass ahead. The truck slammed its brakes. Mr. and Mrs. were too slow to react. Or perhaps they were politely chatting over the day's social activities.

Valerie was inconsolable until he slipped her a note one morning. "The show must go on." Bodies entangled, she whispered, "Now I know why God sent an actor to fulfill my life."

Of course, now it seemed like so much mawkish crap, but then she was magic and he felt like her savior. Valerie insisted that her parents' wedding bands, retrieved from the wreck, become Cal's and hers. She had them resized. Her parents' engraving remained, "1939. Our love." He used to worry that he'd get hit by a bus, with no identification upon him, and the ambulance workers examining his ring would be astounded by how well preserved a body he had.

Stop reminiscing Calvert. That was years ago. And here we are, dressing for yet another charity event. Yes, here we are. But this one will be different. Yes it will.

peeking at the peep

Maura's heart finally slowed down. Hailing the cab, she had thought the thumping pumping would erupt from her brain and missile shoot into the starless sky leaving her in a heap at the curb. But a taxi pulled up and she calmly gave the driver the 18th Street address.

To all intents and purposes, I appear normal. Do I? Can the driver sense – no, he barely looked at me. Like everyone. Every man. Banish that thought, Maura. Tonight you will be looked at. Maybe even looked at with desire.

The description of the "party" was embedded in her brain. How many times had she pored through the what-to-do magazine, the what-to-do-in-the-underground-sex-world-of-nyc magazine? It was the only risqué event mentioned in the magazine that she felt qualified to attend. Most were for couples only. Unqualified. Some were for swingers. Also unqualified. But this one, the Peep Peek Peak Party, that one had her name on it. Call and make a reservation to obtain the address. Women admitted for a reduced fee. Couples pay. Unattended men — did I say un-attended? Unaccompanied men paid a hefty price. No equality here. No solicitation. BYOB. They provide the mixers. Dress to undress. Coat check and clothes to be checked securely by an attendant. Private party room provided. A privacy notice to be signed at the door and a pledge not to push your desires where they're not wanted. Will I find my desire when I don't even know what that is? But all the rules and caveats calmed her. This was a professional operation. No flakes here. No sleaze. Maura, you are allowed to go.

Now, how do I actually dress to undress? Just plotting her wardrobe was exciting. Strangers will see me. Touch me. She shifted against the taxi seat. The nubby wool of her boxy black coat tickled her through her worn denim shirt dress, a deliberate disposable which she planned to stuff into her now folded shopping bag upon arrival. Underneath the dress, she wore a black lace tube top with her nipples very visible and a black lace thong. Black thigh high stockings climbed up her long legs. I look good. I look hot. I feel hot.

For the BYOB, she had filled her grandfather's old tin flask with tequila. Probably the first time it's been used since the nineteen fifties. Maura had had two shots of tequila before she left her apartment. I can still taste the chasing lemon on my lips. Gus. The first time we did shots, you said you wanted to fuck my brains out. Gus. Right in the middle of a conversation about Scrabble and our mutual passion for the game.

Outside the window of the cab, she saw a couple waiting for the light, arms around each other. Now I think maybe marriage is only an interruption of someone's life. My life. I think it's time to stop idolizing Gus. He didn't love me. He was with me but he didn't love me. All those years and me— ? A hamster lover desperately spinning for want of love. I don't feel that desperate hunger any more. Thank you, God.

Indeed, when the grief of losing him had passed, she finally felt some peace. No one to please. No one to give her that critical look and make her feel stupid. No one to make her feel safe. As unhappy as she was, Gus had made her feel safe. Maybe that's what keeps you alive now, being on guard, never safe, always on your toes. Or maybe that's what gives me the ability to take flight. Tippy toes. Nothing to lose. What's up there? Over the hill. On the top shelf. Waiting for me. Waiting for me. Come and get it.

Retreat at your own peril.

I can no longer retreat. I am a blind woman reckless with no cane. Oh boy, do I feel good. Please God, let this feeling last.

correspondence interruptus

Dear Teenie,

Did I tell you? I got a job as a concierge.

(Yeah right. You're a bell boy, man. A bell boy. Bell bell hop hop to it boy!)

Come to think of it, I wrote you about this last time, didn't I? Well, I got the job. They saw me and said, "You're hired." It's a really trendy boutique hotel downtown. It's so damn exclusive, it's got no name on the front awning. Just NN. No name – get it? Pretty fly when you think about it. I tell the tourists, the Guests, where to go in town.

(Even if I was the concierge, where do I know where to go? I haven't even gone to the top of the World Trade Center or the Empire State Building or that Natural History Museum and I've been here how long? You're an embarrassment Chester. There I go. Calling up the old name. The loser boy. I'm no loser now. I'm Chet.)

I tell them what's hot like music, clubs and stuff.

(I drag their bags with a smile. Don't these Eurotrash know I live for tips? I like that new word. Eurotrash. Makes me feel cool just saying it. Study those Eurotrash, Chester Chet. Yeah, good study for an actor. Their hips go into the room before their heads. Their lips curl in some weird no smile at you bell hop invisible boy.)

He stops writing. What can I write her? She thinks I'm in magic land. She's the one in magic land. Orlando sun and friends and family at dinner and Mom's famous key lime pie light as air. I'm so hungry all the time.

And that tight assed manager when he hired me.
"I'll be blunt. Sex with a guest is automatic grounds for dismissal. Immediate. No excuses. Got that, kid?"
"Yes, sir."
"I like you. You'll do well here."
And the fucker winks. Winks.

Chet placed the big black suitcase on the luggage rack. Just today. He opened the room door and laid the suitcase on the luggage rack. I follow all the rules. The corners of the bag were shiny brass. Not a scratch or a dent. I bet this guy rides private planes or first class all the time.

The closely bearded man pulled a bill from his pocket and walked toward Chet. He folded the bill smaller and smaller with every step.

You're coming into my space. Too close. Too close. Grounds for dismissal.

Chet turned his back to him. Snapped up the TV remote control and pressed the power button on.

Just checking that it works, sir. You can ring down to the desk for anything you need.

The man slipped the bill into Chet's side pants pocket and let his hand stay there. The disembodied hand. His middle finger probed downward towards Chet's cock. Chet pivoted around ejecting the man's hand from his pocket.

Thank you, sir. Enjoy your stay.

Pfft. Out the door. The bearded man stood there. The bill still in his hand.

With the door safely shut behind him, Chet confirmed what he already knew. He looked down at the bulge in his pants. Deep regular breaths until it went down.

Dear Teenie,
  The guests here.... The guests here......

He stopped writing.

Sometimes the guests stiff me for tips. Yeah, very funny, Chet.

chit chat amidst the clink of crystal

Cal took a sip of the scotch as he left the open bar. So many people, no one will notice I neglected to leave a tip. He glanced around the room. Valerie was deep in conversation with a tall, massive woman so glittery in her dress that Cal thought she resembled a walking Christmas tree. He didn't recognize the snow globe queen. I imagine that Val is rounding up new clients. Ever busy, she.

Well, I shall be busy as well. True, my first attempt with that prudish Monroe Vincene Cabell was not exactly successful but I still have Valerie's rolodex. A veritable abundance of potential clients. My clients.

Ah, a familiar face is heading my way. We had dinner. When? Maybe three, four months ago. Val, myself, his wife. Name. Name begins with an "S." Schuyler. Yes, Schuyler Titus. A major insurance executive who dabbled in theater financing. The fantasy that titillates the bank books of so many. The fantasy of being an angel for a breakout play and doubling, tripling the millions they made in less glamorous endeavors. Like insurance. Insurance, the guaranteed cash cow of an industry many suspect as morally bankrupt, feeding off the possibilities of tragedy and then creating beggars at the less than friendly corporate door. Well, a toast to hoping that Schuyler Titus embraces that description — morally bankrupt. Not like puritanical Monroe whose distaste was positively palpable through the telephone line.

Cal followed the trajectory of Schuyler's eyes. Perfect. He marches up to him. Extends his hand.

G. Calvert Blessing. Valerie's husband.
Oh, yes. We had dinner.
That we did.

Cal nods toward the young woman Schuyler had been eying. Her twenty-year-old debutante breasts pillowed out of her dress.

Delightful are they not? There truly is nothing like young breasts happy to air themselves in public.

Schuyler raised his bushy grey eyebrows at Cal's comment. A bridge had been crossed. A brotherhood established.

Shall we raise a glass to the blossom of bosom?

Cal held his scotch aloft but Schuyler hesitated.

A distant memory.

Distant. Just the response Cal had hoped to hear. That slight ring of timidity in his voice. Too timid to call an escort. Too timid to go to a private club. Probably too timid to even watch pornography. Buy it. Rent it. Fearful for his high profile life scurrying under the microscope of these hideous charity galas. Cal leaned into Schuyler's ear. Placed a conspiratorial comforting hand on his money tuxedoed shoulder.

What if I told you I knew something that could come to you, Schuyler? Home delivery. A show.
A show?
The actual act, my friend. No simulation. And young breasts. Real breasts. You watch. They perform.
Penetration?
If you want. A private performance for you alone. Or Dolly, as well, if you like.
Well, I think Dolly might just want it too. Very interesting. I don't believe I've ever heard of such a thing.

Cal gauged his reaction. Saw the wheels of desire turning in his brain.

It is, of course, of considerable expense. These young people are risking their reputation. As am I. But you would be helping them further their educations. Think of it as another charity event.

Nice touch, Cal. Yes yes yes. Reel in that visceral charitable response.

Ten thousand. Plus my twenty percent fee.
So the kids get eight and you get two?

Ever the businessman even in heat. Cal knows Schuyler knows this was not some random information he's passing along out of the goodness of his heart. Cal juggles in his brain. How can I make him feel that he is getting a deal when he knows that he is not? How can I make this happen again and again until I no longer care about the spousal allowance? Damned if I'm giving away an extra two thousand that could be mine. But if I get this one under my belt.

Very well. Ten then, total. With my twenty percent included. But it's usually on the top and will be in the future. Consider this an introductory special. The performers are good acquaintances with bright futures in the theater. Students, in fact. I know they would be glad to meet a theatrical entrepreneur such as yourself. Glad to get their feet in the door. As well as other assorted body parts. For you, I could persuade them to take just the eight with the caveat that you consider furthering their careers.

Wink. Wink.
They share a practiced wolfish chuckle.
Yes, Calvert, something to consider.

Schuyler thinks what if it wasn't just Dolly and me? Maybe two or three other couples? They've joked about this kind of thing. Well, not exactly this kind of thing. But they've reminisced about the sixties. Longed for all the things they'd read about and missed. Orgies and the like. House keys tossed into a serving dish. Let's see. Who? Maybe the Heinzes? What about Harvey and Mariella? Sandro and Charlotte? No, she's too much the chatterbox. He was born in Spain, though. A European. Broadminded and all. Oh, I should invite my cousin Ott. Definitely Ott and his wife Kitty. Not including us, six is max for security. The building. The doormen. Do I give them an extra tip? No, that would be a red flag.

A second had passed and already the guest list was complete in Schuyler's head. A miracle of neural connectors.

Have you organized something like this before?
A little thing I do sometimes.

The first time and it better be good. How shall I coach them? How shall I keep them in the dark? Calvert, you do not even officially have a "them." He put his hand on Schuyler's forearm.

A little thing I do sometimes. For friends.
And Valerie? Does she know?
Valerie has her business and I have mine. We keep things separate. I assure you, she is totally unaware. Literally unaware.
But I'm her client.
Schuyler, I am trusting in your discretion. From the time we met, I felt an immediate kinship with you.

Yes, the kinship of dollars and sex. Oh I do feel wonderful. Cal and Schuyler clinked glasses in a toast. The scotch momentarily caught in Cal's throat. I have placed the cart before the horse. No matter. This I can do. I know it.

upstairs

Once inside, once paid for, she climbed the steep inner staircase of the 18th Street townhouse. A door opened into a big empty space rid of all previous walls. The few support columns were covered in glitter. Somewhere a DJ was playing dance beat music. Maura checked her coat, shed her denim dress into her shopping bag and checked that too. Her chest went concave. She shrunk into herself. What am I doing here? And it's cold.

Maura looked around. The room was half full with an odd assortment of people, most of them less than attractive. Most of them couples. It was quiet save for the music and laughter was non-existent. Maura remembered the flask and hurried to retrieve it from the shopping bag. She headed over to the makeshift bar.

Various liquor bottles were lined up with names taped to them. Idiot. I should've stopped in a store and bought a pint. The bartender eyed her flask.

Don't worry, Sweetie. I won't let it get lost. Whaddya want with that?
You have any orange juice?

Of course.
That flask was my grandfather's. I feel stupid that I brought it here.
The bartender put her plump hand on Maura's.
Nobody does nothing stupid here. Relax. Have fun. Next time, bring your grandpa.

Paper cup in hand, Maura felt comfortable enough to wander around the room. Some couples were dancing. Everyone was wearing their idea of sexual whether it was cut-out or leather or fur or whatever. A pear-shaped hairless guy asked her to dance. She just shook her head and said, "later." No excuses here. No one knows me here. Even I don't know me here.

Over in the corner, a man lay across a narrow beige formica kitchen table. His face was hidden below a black leather mask and there was a gag in his mouth. His hands were tied to the table legs and he was naked except for black and orange striped socks. The socks were actually the first things that had caught Maura's eye. A red-haired woman in full dominatrix gear hovered over him. Maura walked closer to see what exactly they were up to. Wasn't part of the name of the party "peep?" Then I shall. Peeping Maura examining another side of life.

The dominatrix grasped some kind of electrical stimulation gadget that she aimed at the man's penis. It made a crackling zizzy sound and he jerked at its touch, then moaned. The gadget was applied again. Not me. No. I would not want to be at the receiving end of that thing.

A twosome in matching khakis and blue button-down Oxford shirts passed by her and gave her a smile. Where did they come from? Did they get lost from a tour bus?

Dance, pretty lady?

A rolling, weighty young girl with bulbous bare breasts and paper clips on each of her nipples offered her hand to Maura. Maura put down her drink and followed her out onto the floor. The beat was fast enough that their bodies could be distant. The young girl shimmied with every move and Maura felt her thong moisten as she imagined being cradled between those breasts, her tongue finding nipples as hard as hers.

Then over the girl's shoulder, Maura saw them walk in. The two men were wearing tuxedos and one carried a briefcase. The other held a double leash attached to the necks of two copper-haired women who looked remarkably alike even though their heights differed radically.

The dance ended and Maura made a polite thank you. She drifted away with her drink to position herself against a brick wall. She knew exactly what she wanted to watch now.

valerie eyes

She had seen the short, white-haired black man sitting in the lobby of the hotel when they entered from the cold and his very presence soothed her. He was the same man she had seen drinking coffee in a car parked by their building. She was looking for him and she thought, yes, this must be him. Would he come up from the lobby? Would he survey the gala?

Monroe Cabell had called her early last week.

I hate to bother you, Valerie, but our business ties go way back and I would hate for them to fray. I could be the only one he contacted but, honestly, my gut tells me "no."
Monroe? What— ?
It's your husband. This could jeopardize your business rep or I wouldn't be calling. I struggled with this. Marriages are crazy, I know, but business.

And I panic, panic, panic. What has Cal done? What has he said? How dare he contact Monroe. Anyone. These are my people. My life. He's supposed to stay at home and come out when I fucking say so.

Is it worse than I imagined? She listened to Monroe's tale. No. Almost laughable. But dangerous. Bizarre. She thanked him for the heads up. Thanked him for letting her know hell was beckoning.

Monroe's voice grew deeper on the phone. He oozed empathy. Empathy she didn't want to have anything to do with.

For what it's worth, Valerie, I gave him a piece of my mind.
Thank you. Thank you, Monroe.

You think you're my savior? I never want to do business with you again. Thoughts and thoughts and the big unknown. I don't like thinking like this. It's messy. I like things tidy. Calvert you must be insane. Not only do I need these people to generate income but they are the ones I approach for my charities. Cal, you rip the threads of my web and I'll take the scissors to you.

She called her lawyer of the big belly and wood paneled walls.

David, I know you must have in-house investigators at the firm. May I borrow one?
A silence. Then acceptance.
I will make the arrangements Valerie. I don't want you dealing directly. If this is marital, I want your hands clean. Is it marital? Should I refer you—
No. At the fringe, if that's an answer. Please David, no questions. Just let me give you the target.
For you, for now, no questions. But down the road.

Down the road.

on the irt

Bibi easily found a seat on the subway. The dentist appointment kept her shy of the morning rush hour. So nice to find a seat, read a book, drift away. She pulled the biography of Marie Curie out of her tote. For years now, she'd been devouring biographies, trying to imagine her life in the lives of others, transform her life, find anything even remotely resembling hers in those of famous folk. No, none of them got my life. But a lot of them come from dust and look where they go.

The train came to a stop. Bibi paid no attention to those getting on. She was in France.

Then a raspy voice broke her calm.

I don't steal. I don't rob. I swear on the eyes of God, I don't do this normal. I'm just hungry. Anything you got. Anything at all.

Usually Bibi let the panhandlers become background music on the subway. But that voice. This day. The stench grew closer. Sweat and piss. And Bibi looked up.

Bibi? Bibi, that you? Oh, Dios mio, mi niña!

Bibi was suddenly engulfed in scabby arms, being kissed by chapped lips. Dried spittle flaked onto her coat and blouse collar. The woman shrieked with joy.

Bibi!

Everyone in the car looked her way. Oh, no. I'm going to smell like her at work. She tried to extract herself from the choking embrace.

I'm not Bibi.
Oh, yes. Bibi. Bibi. Bibi. I know you don't want to know. I did bad by you. But it weren't me. Papi Fannon he picked you up six months old. Kissy on the hootch like all Papi's do to make the babies laugh. Even though you wasn't his for real. I love him but then he say, "Look, the kid like it. She like it a lot. We can make some money here."

Bibi felt all the eyes, all the ears, all the gossipy brains of everyone in the subway car. They knew. They know. They all knew this was her mother.

Stop, already. Everyone can hear you.
Okay, I whisper, Bibi, only you and me. It was Fannon. Fannon, he put a spell on me. He bring the misters into our lives. Kiss me, Bibi.

The train found its station. The doors opened.

Mami, no! Get away.
Bibi my angel!

Bibi threw her off and ran for the door. She pushed and ran up the subway steps despite knowing Mami was probably still on the train, still hustling for coin. Bibi seethed to run away from her heart, the stench, the smell of burnt emotion long gone into ash. Once on the street, sobs climbed up from her belly and wallowed from her mouth. Her body folded over itself. Bibi's knuckles fairly popped, she gripped the subway stair rail so tightly. The air was cold. I can breathe. I didn't see her. That didn't happen. She didn't happen. Nothing happened. I'm going to work. I have a new filling from the dentist that I paid for with money I earned at a desk and.....

A breeze moved the air and once again she smelled Mami the octopus all over her. Bibi passed a Bolton's and rushed in and onetwothree bought a new white blouse to wear to her job and some cheap cologne to spray on her coat. She tossed the subway blouse in the trash.

A bus pulled up. The journey to the office continued. Bibi got on, opened the Marie Curie book. It wasn't easy but with enough concentration, she crossed the ocean to France once more. She imagined herself working hard in a laboratory, teaching her daughters Polish, the mother tongue, and then winning a Nobel Prize. That's a big life. That's a life. At the next stop, a child climbed the bus steps screaming at his mother. "I don't wanna! I won't! I just won't." And Bibi wondered why she was such an angel she never said no. It hurt to make sense of it. I won't never make sense of it. She crept back into her imagination and let the bus take her away.

Everything be done now and she was the last of it, Mami was. I got no more goodbyes to make. Hey, you got no more goodbyes, then what you got? She smiled as she pulled up the word. Pulled it up from hours of studying for her GED. Antonym. You got the antonym of goodbye, Bibi De Los Santos.

dangerdanger

It was one of those days Cal dreaded. One of those days that made him feel old. Snow, rain, sleet the night before and now the radio said black ice ruled the sidewalks. Cal was terrified of falling.

I am old enough to break a hip. Anyone is old enough to break a hip but to break a hip now when a new beginning lies before me. The stuff of a Shakespearean tragedy. Calvert, you exaggerate. But still, they say the hip bone breaks first and then you crumble to the ground. Question the fall. Blame the fallen. Bones so brittle, they just disintegrate. A lifetime of antacids and you must pay the price. Ah, reflux. Bones as chalky as Tums. No, those are the bones of old women. Those are my bones. My bones broke the gender statistical rules of bone density scans and the doctor even smiled at that announcement.

I shall keep a sharp eye. I shall watch for people, youngsters especially, who might bump into me. I shall wear my lumberjack shoes even though they spoil the break of my trousers.

And those plastic death traps. Plastic death loops. The strapping for newspapers and parcels. He remembered that day last spring when he was walking, appreciating a juicy glowing girl with no sense of attention to the plastic loop awaiting him on the sidewalk. One foot in, then the other. He never realized he was encircled until he went down like a stone, face first on the sidewalk. Blood from his nose, his cheek.

Sir, can I help you?

It was the juicy girl. Small favors from an unknown god. But at the same time as she offered assistance, her young cellphone fingers had already connected with 911.

I'm calling because an old man fell.

Old man? Old man. Cal struggled to get up.

I am perfectly fine. Do not tell them to come. I will not even be here. I need no assistance.
Well, I was just trying to help.
And that you have.

He marched down the street to get away from her. Hailed a cab to go home to clean the blood and shame and sadness from his face. You just wanted to help, did you? Help me see what I do not care to see? Calling me an old man. I do not consider that help.

Cal put that memory aside. The anger hurt. He was tired of all the anger within him. Go away. Go away.

He opened the door of the building and the cold air went straight for the target of his exposed face. Now I have two things to be wary of — black ice and plastic loops. I have good peripheral vision. I can do this.

But all his peripheral vision revealed was a shivering Pammy, hovering two doors down and well over an hour before class.

Are you stalking me?
No.

But her stomach fell into a clutch and her nose itchy tingled like before she was going to cry. Because she was. Because she was stalking. Because she was hoping to see him exiting the building opening his mail. Opening her postal touch. Smiling at all the wonderful doors she had opened for him. But there was no smile on Calvert's face now and her tears tensed at her lashes.

I have an appointment down the block to get my legs waxed. I'm early.
You appear to be early with some frequency.

Did he know? Had he seen her by the dumpster? By the tree?

Oh, it's time for me to go now.

Pammy walked to the waxing place. She knew his neighborhood too well now. Yes, they accepted walk-ins. No, she had never had her legs waxed before. She barely shaved and certainly never shaved the backs of her legs because she couldn't see them. And besides, who was looking? She took off her elastic waist brown polyester pants. She lay down on the paper covered table. Hey, that hurts. That hurts. The song in her head. What I did for love.

Cal didn't look at me any differently. Not like he'd thought of me at all. Well, he doesn't know that he's thinking of you, Pammy. You didn't tell him you're the one that the mailman's been delivering. The girl in disguise. The girl with only you in her eyes.

And Calvert continued on his mission. He bought the half-gallon of two percent milk in the corner deli. Milk that only Valerie used but was too busy to buy. How much longer shall I play this role? I am not your personal assistant, your shopper.

A short, white-haired black man was selecting flowers from the half-frozen ones at the front of the store. Cal passed him on his way out. People are so foolish. Is he not capable of seeing their obvious decay?

He went into a small heel skid on that thought but didn't fall. Focus, Calvert. Negativity makes your mind less sharp. And, of course, all the authorities now declare that it impacts your health as well. And, that is all I need.

and you up up up one stair two

Maura climbed the stairs to Loft D to the sanctuary of Cal. This climb is nothing, to nowhere. My climb at 18th Street. That was an education. All these days and I can't stop thinking. Can't stop wishing for some miraculous sensory recall of the exact way that rope felt between my legs.

The two men and the two women had entered the party and walked directly to a support column on the right side of the room. As if someone had mailed them a map. As if they had been there before. Had been to places like this hundreds of times, thousands. The women removed their long, red wool princess coats. Below, they wore matching red lace teddies. As they turned about, Maura could glimpse slivers of their surprisingly white buttocks. Are mine that white? No, nothing could be that white. Do they have make up on down there? Rice flour for a surreal Geisha ass?

The older man with the white mustache and goatee removed the leashes on the two women. Their collars remained. He carefully folded the women's red coats and walked them over to be checked. The younger man knelt by his briefcase, snapped it open and reverently, religiously, lifted a package the size of an infant from within. It appeared to be wrapped in black velvet. He carefully opened it to reveal a hank of rope, maybe two. Maura wasn't sure which. The young man stood up and approached the column. By then, the older man had returned. Maura immediately noticed the women stood somewhat straighter. They belong to him. They are his property. He is their keeper. The thought did something to her blood. Something new.

The younger man slowly wrapped the ropes into various knots and around the column. He extended the ropes to about twelve feet from the column and held one end in each of his hands. Then he knelt on one knee and bowed his head. Every move was a living pause, ritualistic and feline in grace. The older man leaned over and kissed him atop his head. Only then did the young man look upward. On cue, the taller of the two women straddled the ropes. The younger man stood up and as he did, the ropes rose to the height of her vagina. With each hand, he began to rhythmically toss the ropes in opposite directions, up and down. He flicked his wrists and every movement that shimmied down the ropes caused the woman to shiver in ecstasy. The rope dance heightened until she had an orgasm. Right there in front of everyone. Right there in front of Maura.

The rest of the room barely paid attention. The party was in full swing and getting noisy. But Maura was transfixed. I want to feel that. How can a rope do that? A thing so rough, so harsh.

Maura downed the rest of her drink and walked over to them, to the young man.

Can I join you? Can I do that?
The young man's eyes shot towards the white-haired gentleman for permission. A nod was received.

Hi, I'm Maura.

The threesome stared at her. Not a smile. No expression. Did I commit a faux pas? Maybe you don't exchange names at these things. Or you use made up names.

The older man took her hand.

Be calm. I am Netov. This is Chartreuse and Manzanilla and the young Monsieur Apollinaire.
Like the poet?
Oui, Madame Maura, like the poet. It is commendable that you are acquainted with him. Our Monsieur Apollinaire, however, is a poet of the ropes.
May I touch them?

The young man rested one rope in her hand. It was weightless.

It is the purest silk. The highest quality. I have them specially woven to my taste. No matter for what purposes I might use them, they will never leave a mark. Never burn a woman's softest, most delicate skin.

Monsieur Apollinaire leaned in closer to Maura. His breath smelled like cinnamon.

My ropes are meant to caress your thighs, your very self. Please,

I beg of you. Take a step over them.

Maura stood there as he slowly raised the ropes. Her thong covered her vagina but somehow she felt the ropes were dancing across her bare skin. Monsieur Apollinaire changed the tempo of the dance. Maura could feel her clitoris harden and reach out toward the silken ropes, begging to be touched. It grew difficult to stand. She wanted to be lying down to experience such pleasure. Her knees bent slightly. The concentration to stand added to the act. Her body was warming. Her nerve endings were joining forces with her clit. A small sound escaped her. The ropes were moving faster, kissing her thighs, her juices flowed. Maura had no thoughts for the party, for the people, even the rope people. She was within herself, exploding. It was a climax like she'd never had before.

And then she opened her eyes. She was just standing there, sweaty. The music that she couldn't hear before seemed suddenly loud. Netov, the women and Monsieur Apollinaire were close by. Monsieur Apollinaire looked at her without even a suggestion of a smile.

You did enjoy?
Thank you. Thank you.

They were all looking at her. She didn't know what to do. Do we have small talk now? Dance? None of them smile and I can't stop. What do I do? What do I do?

Thank you. I've got to go now.

And she did just that. Knocking into people to get to the makeshift coat check room. Racing down the stairs, almost tripping. Hailing a cab. Realizing her grandfather's flask was still upstairs and she would never see it again.

And now, here I am going once more to this stupid, stupid class of Cal's. I do everything wrong. That was rude of me at the party. We could have exchanged numbers. Become close personal friends. Maybe they have special rope parties. Maybe they have a collar with my name on it. Maybe. That feeling, the rope, it was like a drug. Like a first high, never to be retrieved as gloriously again. But you blew it. You blew it, Maura.

Anton came bounding up the stairs and plowed by her.

Anton, slow down.
I am sorry. I have news. I have news.

air matters

George, you and Pammy shall do it together today. I believe she needs your guidance.

Pammy's eyes fairly popped onto the floor.

Are we?

Are we what, Miss Pammy? Could it be you do not have clean underwear on? Did not your mother always give you that just-in-case warning? No, my mouse. You should be able to identify a tease and greet it with laughter. Erase the terror from your face and attend to the air mattress for that is what I am referencing. George, she is your charge.

Obediently, George moseyed over to the cardboard box that held the air mattress and plugged in the pump to blow it up. Pammy wondered how Calvert knew about Mother.

Cal watched George go through the ritual with Pammy standing behind him like a stick. How many years ago did I start this? Perhaps even the first year. A delicious touch. Somewhat delicious, somewhat mysterious. I am a man of principles. I have never asked any student to lie on it. During class, that is. But there, just off center in the room, it looms. It terrifies all of them.

It terrifies Calvert as well. A strangely solid piece of real estate recognizable as an abyss. Yes, I am afraid of it. Afraid to cross the line. To have them sprawled about prone would be just one step beyond sleaze. I will not go there. He will not go there. Could not, would not go there. I am a fraud but I am not that. It is a prop. Yes, it is a prop to remind all the boys and girls that — what? That that could be in their future, looming not here but on a set, on a stage. Not as some college crashing roomie come to town from the sticks, but yes, as a decision they will someday have to make. To lie down or not to lie down. Oh, I love it even more. How steeped in symbolism I have become in my older age. Cal patted himself on the back. Yes, I am a sly devil and intelligent without even thinking about it. Just naturally brilliant.

He looked around the room. This is a class in procrastination. I hold onto them for six weeks, teach them nothing and pray they do not get wise until the six weeks have passed. Shadows and light. Fraud and procrastination.

mashpee roots

The mattress. The mattress. Wissa stared as George pumped it up. Oh, mattresses.

She grew up in Mashpee on Cape Cod. Dad was a carpenter and a poet and he transformed a barn into our house. The money found his hammer not his words. And those words became lamentations. The story she knew for as long as she could remember. How his college friend Sandy, the lead singer of the group Hot To Fox, stole his lyrics.

How'd he steal your lyrics, Daddy?
He copied them out of my poem book. He took the music right out and guitared them up and went to an agent. Claimed they bore no relation.

Mommy looks up at the sky, looks up a the ceiling, looks up at anything whenever the story begins. And her small sentence slips out.

Bore no relation as in bore as in boring.
You think a gold record doesn't count for something?

Then why didn't you write more songs? More poems people could use as lyrics? And show Sandy who's who.
Because I'm a poet. A free verse poet. That was sophomoric stuff. Case closed. Road closed. Dead end.

Who even remembers Hot To Fox? I certainly don't. Not around when I was growing up. Even later, in yard sales, I never saw their records. Not one.

Mommy, did Hot to Fox exist?
Of course, Wissa. Briefly.
Was this Sandy guy really a thief?
Mom looked off as if the outdoors were calling her.
He was very sweet.

Dad was a carpenter and he made a barn our house. He hammered and drew and hammered and drew and the smell of sawdust became my favorite smell. We pitched a tent in the middle of the barn floor and peed under the stars. I was the happiest nine-year-old. And when he was finished, the great center was still open to the room but now a balcony encircled all. A balcony with bedrooms and closets and book shelves and odd cubby holes and occasional stairs to no-where, just because.

It was a beautiful home but hot. All year long the hot air rose up into the bedrooms. I was supposed to be asleep but snuck out of my room, opened my door to sit on the balcony landing. I just wanted to feel the center cooling fan blow air against me, under me, over me. I tucked my little self behind the railings. No one can see me. No one can see me. I was ten.

That was the year the parties began. I could see them below, milling about at first. All Mommy and Daddy's friends. The Duggans. The Perls. Buddy Popkin and his girlfriend Cass. Mom's oldest friends from childhood, Amy Losavia and her husband Victor. At first, I thought they must be hot too, with shirts off and then more shirts off. And then the mattresses appeared. Where did they come from? I have no idea.

Mom saw me once and shooed me back into my room. I wasn't stupid. It didn't take me long to figure out the clothes were off to get them hotter.

I heard them once, Mom and Dad, talking before breakfast.
But not us. Don't want her to see us.
Best, most natural education she could get.
But not us.
Then you just be discreet, Angie. Discretion being your middle name.
What does that mean?
Not like you to ask the obvious.

I was twelve and hiding, watching the party, the mattresses, the bodies entangled, the laughter, the moany noises. Two years now and I think they knew I was there. Didn't mind or wanted or maybe even excited by a witness. And then Victor Losavia looked up and caught my eye squeezed up against the oak railings and he smiled. I had to smile back. I had to. He was our next door neighbor. He was one of Mom's oldest friends since they were kids and his wife Amy taught me how to bake sugar cookies. I had to smile back.

Victor was a leather worker. He made belts and wallets and sandals and bags for a shop in Provincetown. His fingers were thick and stained from dye. Even the rusty Buick he rode back and forth to P-Town was stained where he touched the doors.

I walked over the next day to his work shed. Just next door. The Losavia's were always in our lives. From every day I could remember. And he was standing there in his leather work apron and no shirt and the curly hair dancing up over the top and he said, Wissa, I've been waiting for so long for you to finally come visit me and then he shut the door and took away the sun.

a sound class

Very well class, today we will emote.

The door to the loft swung open and Anton stomped in with Maura just behind him. Anton waved his hands wildly.

I am to explode. I must to tell you all. I must.

His smile made them all uncomfortable. Even more so than the mattress in the center of the room. That smile of his — too broad, too full of joy. It knocked them aside and bullied them for air.

Please, sir, Mr. Blessing. I must to speak.
Well, if you must, you must, Anton. The floor is yours.
Yesterday, I am in my street where I live.

He had seen the no parking signs taped to the lamp posts the day before yesterday. Every New Yorker knows what they mean. A film, a commercial, a tv series shooting on location and your street, the grit or glitz of your neighborhood is A number one perfecto immaginata. The fantasy realized. Your every day is some big so-and-so's money dream. Anton read the details on the sign carefully. The production was for “Dark Allies” a well-known espionage tv series in its thirteenth season. Almost every working New York actor had found a part in its scripts or had auditioned or hoped to audition. Everyone knew the show, even Anton who didn’t even own a television set. It was New York to the core, steeped in politics, the intrigues and moral lapses of diplomats, the cocktail party machinations of United Nations delegates. Like any self-respecting wannabee, Anton felt excitement and purpose just reading the sign, knowing they would be in front of his building.

Still in his bed in the basement in the wee hours of today’s most auspicious morning, he could hear the trucks pulling into the empty parking spaces and the occasional voices of the crew. By dawn, Anton was dressed, kneeling at his bed, praying to every saint he could remember.

At seven-thirty, he opened the door to his building and surveyed the activity on the street. The big lights. All the things they piled and hung around them on stands that he did not understand. Why do they stretch that shiny fabric? Why the railroad track there? The people. So busy. They are all so busy and not so busy. This one does that. And that one, he holds that little glass high and stares at the one cloud in the sky. And why is that woman to wet the street with a hose on the first dry day all week? None of this I understand but all of this I want to be in.

And then I see not far away a man with a small cart and he is wearing headphones. He talks to a pretty girl with braids. I think she is a pretty girl and headphones she hold too. Them I will speak to. And I do. And I ask who is famous here today and can I work? And you know, he laughs, the man. She says, that's not how it goes, my friend.

And then I have the idea immediately. It is in my head like that. I say in my most big voice, the voice of opera. I say, "I AM HERE TO WORK." And everyone on the street, they look at me. At me, Anton. "I AM HERE TO WORK."

A man in a cap, he comes over and he ask me am I extra or principal.
I am here to work. I am Anton Grybowski.
And the man, he talk small into a walkie talkie. I hear him. I hear — principal. I hear — Anton Grybowski. My name.
He say to me — This character is not anywhere on the call sheet today. Or tomorrow. He ask am I being on the right shoot. He say there are movie people also on Lenox Avenue. And then he stop. I see he listen to the thing in his ear.
He say — Wait. Wait. They want to see you.

And they take me to where a fat man sit. He wear all blue, everything, hat, coat, scarf all around the neck and blue shoes. Yes, even that. He is director. This I know. It say this on his chair.
He say — There is no Anton Grybowski in the script, bud. But you got a great voice and chutzpah.
I say — I am Anton Grybowski. This is my name.
And this make him to laugh. And when he laugh, everybody laugh. Everybody.
He say — You are big man, Mr. Grybowski. I like your style. I like the accent. We will use you tomorrow.

And they give me a line. I have a line. I am to come back tomorrow. I am actor.

Everyone in the loft suddenly feels emptiness and despair. Even Cal. That's not how it works. That's fantasy. That's make believe. Totally against the laws of the acting universe. And then they look at the big bull that is Anton and know that he won the lottery and they did not.

The whole room claps for him. Way to go, Anton. Great move, Anton.
Cal offers his professional expertise.
I can coach you. I will always be here to coach any of you students even after the semester is concluded.
Seamus, though, wonders – What is your line, Anton?
My line? Get down you.

How applicable to our class, smiles Cal. Shall we all give that line a go? Each one, his own choice of emphasis. You first, of course, Anton.
Get down you.
Get down you.
Get down you.
Get down you.
Get down you.
Get down you.
Get down you.
Except for the octave, they all sounded the same.

and the minus invisible

Seamus found it unsettling that no one had acknowledged Bibi's absence. Especially Cal. Throughout the ritual of the mattress, the late arrivals of Anton and Maura, the naive gloating of Anton's instant success, Seamus kept glancing at the door, listened for its creak. I should have called after that last class. I should have called her last night. Shoulda woulda coulda. I will call her. I have her number. She gave it to me.

He knew that number was precious and to be respected. He had carefully copied it into his address book. The small dark green miniature book he had chosen for its understatement at the stationery store. The book that was virtually empty.

classified as verbiage or effects

Maura checked her watch. She had checked it two minutes ago but already forgot what it had read. How many times will I have to hear that George say “Oh God?” Cal had moved the class on from Anton’s line in “Dark Allies” to the sound effects of an orgasm. When it was her turn, she had managed something between a grunt and a small sigh.

Is that your best, Ms. Felix?
That’s my most honest.

And did she make any noise at that party? She could no longer remember. Where do I go from 18th Street? Was that akin to taking myself down to some kind of depths or was it simply an eye opener? To what? That I can do anything. Take any risk. But who would know? I’m certainly not telling anyone. But what if someone from there recognizes me walking down the street? What if I see Monsieur Apollinaire the rope man again? Say he just happens to be on the crosstown bus and he recognizes me and we go home to his dungeon and—

An even louder “oh God” rumbled out of George. His eyes were closed. He was thinking of Pammy. Cal just let him go on and on. The truth? All eyes, save Maura's, were now focused on George's crotch. There was no denying the hard-on struggling beneath his dirty jeans.

Pammy stood up.
Make him stop. Make him stop.
And if I do? Cal asked.

But, of course, George and his boner were already silenced. Cal surveyed the room. He had already made mental notes about Wissa and Chet. Notes filed to be relished and, hopefully, embellished.

Well, young George appears to have been stilled mid-performance by the damsel somewhat distressed. Then it must be your turn, Pammy. Please. Give us a squeak or two.

Chet started to laugh but a threatening look from George shut him down.

Pammy sat back in her chair and squeezed her eyes shut. I can do this. If Anton can wake up and be discovered, I can do this. And Mother will be proud. Even though she doesn't even know I'm here, she'll be proud. And if I'm an actress, I'll make enough money that I can pay my sisters to look after Mother instead of me. That would be the right thing after all these years.

She shut her eyes and imagined the boy with the messenger bag in the subway. It had been his bag but at first she thought it was something else. Something else pressing, pressing from behind her. She had read once about special subway cars in France where anything goes, wild things. Was that really true? Or did she read it in the supermarket? Keep on track. Keep on track. Just by stepping into those subway cars, everyone knew they could touch you. Anyone could and they knew you wanted to be touched. She was in a French subway car. I am in a French subway car. That is no messenger bag behind me. His hands are on my hips. He lifts my skirt. My brown cotton skirt. No, my tan felt skirt. Pammy, get back on track. You're in class. I'm in a French subway car.

Her thoughts ran split second fast and she forced, willed, commanded the class out of her consciousness.

Ohhhhhhh.

Everyone was taken aback. Most especially, George. His love had found its justification. I give you my heart, my delicious brown-swaddled flower.

Cal clapped.

A most unexpected surprise, Miss Pammy. Never forget, none of you, should it be time for you to perform, that you are the sexiest person, the sexiest people in the room. They are all watching you. Perhaps not the crew but certainly your audience wants to be you. You are the stars. They want to be you. They want to be you being fucked.

Pammy blushed.

As actors, we find ourselves in a place with limited entrée. Fantasy and reality generally inhabit parallel worlds unless you are a stalker, an actor, maybe a poet, writer, certainly a mystic. Sometimes, sadly, even a politician. There. You see how dangerous such a commingling can be? I repeat those key nouns. Outliers all. Politician, stalker, poet, actor, mystic and—

Calvert hesitated. George raised his hand.

Writer.
Thank you, George. The lesson of the dangers of fantasy reality crossover? Sex on set can lead to, as they say, dangerous liaisons. A heady brew best avoided by children.

This, coming from a pseudo Svengali who propositioned me and probably every other student? Maura checked her watch again. Get me out of here.

Next week is our final class of the semester. There will be no major homework scheduled except for you to review what we have covered and to compose at least four questions that may have personally arisen for you. Very good work, everyone. Anton, please, a moment with you after class.

Chairs scraped against the thin rug. Coats on. Scarves and hats a'bundle, they filed out the door. George shoved his way towards Pammy.

Can I call you sometime? Can I have your number?
Me?

She thought it would be Cal asking her to stay after class. Instead, he asked Anton. Why not me? Didn't you see what I can do? Don't you want to take me to Aruba, take me in your arms? Don't you want to hear me go ohhhh besides you?

Pammy, can I call you?
I have to go home. My mother.

She pushed past Seamus flipping through an address book and headed down the stairs.

I want her. I want her. Didn't Cal say make the bold move? This is my bold move. George pulled a crumpled receipt from his jacket pocket and scrawled his phone number on it. He raced to follow Pammy.

Seamus: Hey, will everyone stop trying to knock me down the stairs?

Pammy, Pammy, wait.
George thrust the paper at her.
My number. Call me.

one last

Anton was half out the door.

I wanted to speak with you.
I forget, sir.
Now that you are truly pursuing an acting career, it is probably best that you continue with your studies.
This study?
Well, yes, my boy.
No.
No? But Anton, that is not a wise decision.
No, I am to act now.
You realize it does not work like that. No one, absolutely no one, goes from nothing to working every day. You must perfect your craft.

Oh, dear lord, did I just say "craft?" This boy is dangerous to my health. Anton opened the loft door to leave. Cal grabbed for his elbow.

I would pay you.
I was feeling losted. But now, no.
Please.

Anton smiled.
Goodbye, old man.

Anton ambled down the stairs. All his soul felt that smile. I never do bad things again.

no divide now

Seamus huddled against the wind and tried to drop a coin into the pay phone. Jammed. Yech. Probably gum or something more gross. He crossed the corner and tried again. The phone rang and rang.

It's probably Cal wondering why I didn't show for class. As if I'd go back. As if I'd go back to anything in my back life again. And you Cal, you fit right in with the back life. Bibi let the phone ring. At least he's not crazy buzzing on my door. That man, he knew where I lived.

Seamus looked at his watch. Where would she be this late? She told me she's a homebody. Maybe I dialed wrong. He dropped in another coin and let the phone ring.

What? He's ringing again. I'm going to tell him get lost. Don't be bothering me. Not if he's going to be calling and calling like this. She picked up the phone.

Hello.
Bibi, are you okay? You didn't come to class.

It took her a second to re-align her gears. To go from anger to the wonder that someone cared. It's Seamus. Seamus is calling me. What do I say? That I messed with Cal for you, for me, for all the old crazy inside me. That everything, everything is just—

Bibi? Did something happen?
I— I saw my mother today.
Your mother?

And then the tears and the sobs and the words all gone.

I can't talk. I can't talk.
What's your address? Give me your address. I'm coming over.

Bibi gave it to him. It was right. He was the right person to know.

always my child

Pammy unlocked the door as quietly as she could. It was a welcome night if Mother was already asleep. If she could pretend for whatever short time that she lived alone. That she was an adult.

She did that a week ago even though Mother was awake. She emptied the mailbox and was surprised to see more mail for herself than Mother. I'm the adult. I get the mail. She flipped through the small envelopes and the two big ones and panicked. Brochures for classes and distant destinations. That type of mail was just too familiar. Not your normal charity plea. This was information. Oh my God, did I fill in my address by mistake instead of Calvert's? No wonder he feels no connection. He doesn't even have a sense that my heart is reaching out to him. Maybe he's never gotten one, not one piece of surprise mail originating from my invisible hand. Oh, Pammy did you mess up? Do I have to start all over again? Then she opened the last envelope and inside was a small pamphlet of recipes using French's Yellow Mustard as the main ingredient. I know I didn't send this to him. I absolutely know. And I don't even like yellow mustard. I like brown. How did these get into my mailbox? Addressed to me.

Tonight, coming home, she flicked on the hall light and was surprised to see her mother sitting in the dark on the living room couch.

Mother, are you okay?
I'm a little cold.
Let's get you into bed.
No. Pammy come here. Come by me.

Ever dutiful, Pammy hurried over.

Pammy, come sit in my lap like when you were a little girl.
I'm too big. I'll crush you.
No, please. Sit in my lap just one more time. I want to hold you. I want to remember.
Mother, no. Please.
Pammy, call me Mommy. Sit in my lap.

Pammy slowly sat in her lap. She concentrated on making her body lighter than air against her mother's bony brittle arms, the flesh hanging off her tired tendons. Her mother's arms encircled her. The neediest of tentacles, the tentacles of memory and loss.

You are the best of daughters, Pammy.
You are the best of moms.

It was a ritual recitation. Pammy kissed her.
Let me get up now, Mommy. I'll crush you. It's time to go to bed.
Pammy extracted herself.

By morning, Mother was dead.

away ice blue beach

I want to think. I need to think.

Wissa had had her voice class in the morning. Fourteen people breathing from their diaphragms, improving posture, enunciating every speeding tongue twister everwas everwillbe. Then rush to the subway on up to Dolan's. From cold air to colder, descending into the IRT crypt. Making mental notes to pick up some toilet paper. Eying the water bug scurrying along the platform, hoping he (why is it always "he"?) doesn't head my way. Dolan's. The nasty couple at table four found an old French fry in their ketchup bottle and demanded their burgers be free. The bus boy "accidentally" bussed her ass again. She spotted Midge, the other waitress, swiping a dollar off one of her tables. Half my tip. But I didn't say anything. She has seniority and a big mouth. Me speaking up could get me fired. Every bathroom moment equaled a quick rehearsal of her lines for scene study class. Run. Do this. Do that. By twelve-thirty she was home in her little apartment, peeling off clothes greasy from the oily air of the bar kitchen. She took a toke of a joint one of her voice classmates had given her, then went to wash up. She tossed her dirty clothes into the toilet and put toothpaste on her toothbrush. Her peripheral vision caught the clothes sogging and sinking into the toilet. Shit. She pulled them out drip drip dripping and draped them over the tub. Shit. Well, not going into the hamper now. At least I didn't pee. I'm so tired. I'm so tired. I'm a hamster on the acting wheel. Thank God, Cal's class is almost at an end.

She had heard about Brighton Beach from a regular at the bar.

It's better than Coney. Sure Coney's got rides and all and the hooplah and shows and Nathan's but Brighton's got quiet and Bay Two. Bay Two, you can sit on the breakers and think. Maybe watch some old farts read their papers and yack in Yiddish or Russian but mostly you can heat up with the sun and think.

I want to think. I need to think. And here I am on the D train, cutting classes that I shouldn't cut, playing sorry I'm sick hooky from Dolan's. I'm going to Brighton Beach. I'm going to walk on the sand in winter. Just the way I did growing up.

The cut of winter air had left the boardwalk almost deserted. Wissa listened to the sound of sand heel toe against the wood with every step she took. She inhaled. Thank you voice class for enlarging my lungs. I am so glad to be away from the sirens and crush of Manhattan. She spotted the breakers up ahead and took the stairs off the boardwalk down to the beach. Sand, God I missed the sand. Her sneakers sank and sand swirled in and over the sides but at eighteen icy degrees, she wasn't about to take them off. She headed towards the water line, to the firmer sand. I'll just sit on those breakers and think. Are all the classes doing anything? I got that one commercial and nothing. It's a year already I've been in the city. More. I don't want to be some dried up old bar waitress limping back to Mashpee. Hi, small town, I'm home.

I'll climb on the breakers and spend an hour or two and then get some coffee and go back to the apartment and then— ! Wissa went flying. Hard fall slap on her back. Black ice an invisible glimmer in the sand. The breath wailing out of her. She lay there staring up at the bluest of skies. No one came by to help her up.

A minute, maybe longer, Wissa turned over and stood up. I think I'm going to be black and blue from that one. No helping hand. She brushed the sand off her back as best she could. I am the helping hand. And that's what I have to do.

She never made it to the breakers. It was a quick round trip on the D train and she was back in Manhattan.

lost in other people's thoughts

Her best friend Nan had died. Heart attack. 1-2-3. The curious thing was that she felt little. A dull sadness. They hadn't even spoken in weeks. After forty-odd years of friendship, Nan was — could she say it – becoming tiresome. I've fallen out of love. These last years, hearing nothing but her Stewie problems and tears. I have problems of my own. When do I get to talk? And when Gus was dying all you did was remind me of his faults, the times he had hurt me, solidified my title as doormat supreme. You think I didn't know that? Didn't love him less? No. I loved him more. I loved you less for reminding me.

And then your Stewie complaints morphed into confidences about your trainer, your trysts. What a cliché. Or was she envious that Nan lay near a body hard in every way? She thought of the men she had met these last years at bars, at classes and cringed at their naked aged bodies. Love handles. Why shouldn't they have love handles? Spare tires? No, they should not. Nan's trainer didn't.

On Saturday, she went to the funeral. So pagan to expose Nan like that. That mask of Nan. A little too much blush. The wrong shadow. She was always so particular. She spent almost every afternoon in high school at the make-up counters in Saks ingesting valuable tips. And now a strange clone of Nan lay packaged in a box with not a single ribbon for sparkle.

Nan's sister and Stewie hugged Maura.
"Too sudden," Maura whispered.
"A blessing though, in that," her sister answered.
"You can ride in our car over to the cemetery," from Stewie.

Maura found a seat in the chapel. Barely listened to the service. A massive sob erupted behind her. A man sniffled incessantly. He sobbed again and sniffed again. Maura dug into her purse for a pack of tissues and turned around to offer them. She knew right away it was the trainer. His suit jacket struggled to cover his biceps as he reached for a tissue.

Thank you.
Are you Tibor?

His eyes widened in confusion. She smiled and turned back in her seat. Would you sleep with me now that she's gone? Just once? I don't have her money. I don't have a lycra outfit. I don't have her discipline to wake up at six and rush to my luxury roof to a gym with shiny machines and waiting you. But I have desire and hips that move and a body that sometimes remembers how to get wet.

After the service, Stewie gestured to her to enter the limo.

I can't.

I don't get it. You can't? This is Nan. Nan.
I just can't go, Stewie.

And Maura walked north on Madison Avenue. Nan's sister and Stewie will never forgive me for that. I will never see them again. Death is when emotions run hard and slights are never forgiven. Goodbye Nan. I am without tears. My eyes scrunch from the sun leaping onto the sidewalk. It's the brunch glory sunshine of an east side Saturday afternoon. A walk into Noah's Ark everywhere she looked. Then she saw a woman in a gray beret, her mouth a drifting down, a grimace cold and frozen. The cemented frown. Don't let that be me. Please God, how do I stop it? I feel so lost. Work is not enough. It's just work. Am I solo perpetuata? Unwanted. A waste of space.

Space. Space. Maura's thoughts flowed to the brief New York Times article that had transfixed her when she read it. She had become obsessed with the story. Thought about it so often that she found herself thinking the thoughts of the old Japanese woman. Maura envisioned the steps that led to some reporter typing away.

> How many times have I made sushi? She carefully spread the sweet sticky rice on the nori. Then she emptied each blue capsule onto the rice. A delicate layer of maki and then a layer of wasabi to hide any medicinal taste. She rolled them with the confidence her mother had given her and made the cuts. Then she packed them up, put on her gray coat and hat and walked the two blocks to the subway. A young man jostled her on the steps because she negotiated each one too slowly for his speeding life. When I was a girl I

would have offered to help. It gave me joy. But no one made that offer today.

She sat on the bench waiting for the train. She opened her parcel and nibbled on the sushi. Ah. A slight hint of bitterness but nothing tastes the same as it used to. She boarded the subway and was grateful to find a seat. She ate the last piece of sushi and carefully covered her mouth lest a stranger see. Her mother would have scolded her for eating in public but no one cared now. The schoolgirls diagonally across from her chattered away and ate their chips.

No one will notice me. No one noticed the granny sleeping in her seat. At the end of the line, the conductor discovered her. She was gone.

Maura read the article and identified in a disconnected way with all the details. The Japanese woman was 102 years old. They found a note in her pocket. I have grown too old to live. I must leave air for a child to breathe and space for a simple butterfly.

Space. I still have quite a ways until I get beyond a hundred years. Look at Nan. Did she wake up that last day with even a suspicion an aneurysm would void tomorrow? But if I do have one hundred years, how do I fill them? Am I even capable of putting some semblance of a smile back on my face? On someone else's? If I walk with a plastered smile am I nothing but a grinning idiot? It hurts to smile. Smile. Smile, Maura. I smile.

And a balding white-haired man, an easy cheer to his pockmarked face, his body thick with years, accompanies his dog down the street. His sausage dog, white muzzled, anxiously tugs on the leash to investigate an urgent smell.

I smile. I am smiling.

The man. He looks at me. At me, Maura Felix. Just winks, he does, and walks on.

Score. I won't be making sushi tonight.

spinning wheels

Cal's homework. I can knock this off in a minute. Between orders. Between three beers on a tray and a welcome to Dolan's with a smile. She grabbed a cocktail napkin from the bar. Okay. Questions I may still have about G. Calvert Blessing's class. What questions, Wissa? Like how is any of that about acting? Or were we all acting as students and you were putting on a great show of being a teacher?

I'm beginning to get a little discouraged. Beginning? Wissa you've been chewing these thoughts since Brighton Beach. The voice class, the scene study class, the commercial workshop, Cal's class. I'm bleeding money. Bleeding and I don't feel like I'm really learning. I want to be totally immersed in acting. I want it to ooze from me, not be squeezed in between work and auditions where I'm just another blond girl and nothing special rips from my soul. I want focus. No distractions. I want to take a full time three year course at a conservatory with dedicated actors. The real thing. I don't want to be around the likes of Pammy, George and Maura. God knows what their motives are. Maybe we're all questionable. Even me. No. I want to be an actor. I really want to be an actor. A good actor. I'm not going to let myself get discouraged. Today I'm back to being me. Lying smiling girl.

But forget it. I don't have that kind of money. Or the luxury not to work and just go to school. And who would even help me? Carpenter dad or tweezer mom? Victor? That great deflowerer of virgins? Yeah, dream on. Dream on. Money. Yeah, buy a lottery ticket or is even that just wasting a tree for pie in the sky? It's all on me. It's all on me. I can do this. Other folks have done this. But how?

Waitress? What's happening with our burgers?

night

Pammy crunched under the covers. It's a little cold. I'm cold. Not just my nose but my shoulders, my arms. If I shut the window all the way, there will be no air. If I had a strong arm, I could turn up the valve in the radiator. The radiator clanged. She heard a sound in the hallway. Is someone trying to get into the apartment? She heard the wind move the blinds. The compressor in the refrigerator turned over. A car door slammed shut in the street.

If I get up, I can put a kerchief around my neck and get some socks on. That always makes me warmer. I'll get up and I'll boil some milk with lots of sugar to make me sleepy. Exactly what I'll do.

She turned on the light in the kitchen. Two cockroaches were motionless on the counter pretending to be invisible. I've never seen a cockroach in here before. I keep a clean house. Mother always insisted I keep a clean house. Have they always come out at night? I don't want to share an apartment with cockroaches. Not with cockroaches. Not when I'm alone. I'm alone. And I've never been.

Almost a week since Mother had passed. Big sisters Connie and Vickie and Steffie had swooped in, insisted on cremation, divided up the jewelry, rejected the silver and left her there to clean up all the empty containers from the Chinese takeout.

There was a hard, dull metallic thump in the street and then the sound of a car alarm. Pammy realized it was a car crash. She heard people yelling and a man, “Call the police. Call the police.”

She didn’t call the police. The police can’t help me. The police can’t help me feeling this empty fear. She went to the closet, rummaged deep in her coat pocket until her hand found the crumpled paper. She straightened it out and dialed the number scrawled on it. Without a glance to the clock, she called George.

a day night under clouds

And here's the big news. Guess who I met today? Think hard, Miss Smart. You got it, your favorite singer in the whole world. And Teenie—She was just as nice as could be in person. A real lady. I would've got you an autograph but she was in a real big rush with lots to do. She said to say get well real soon and she gave me a kiss right on my cheek to send to you. So I'm going to wipe my cheek on this paper. Sorry there's no lipstick but I had to wipe it off because of work and all but you can imagine.
Love you Teenie. Working hard.
Your favorite brother (ha ha – your only brother!) — Chet

Chet didn't wipe his cheek on the loose-leaf paper. He signed his name with a newly practiced flourish. That signature is looking good but damn, I don't like lying . Especially to Teenie. That bitch singer she treated me like ten-day-old greens. And when I asked for an autograph she hadn't got no smile no nothing like the Brazilian princess she claims to be.

I'm going to report you to your manager. This is a five star hotel and I don't need hotel staff hounding me. I am here expecting

privacy and respect. And you can forget getting a tip and no fucking autograph no way.
You're going to report me? It's for my sister, m'am. She's a paraplegic.
Nah, I'm not going report you but I see no reason to upset myself by giving you an autograph either. Get outta my sight, bell boy.

And the way she said "bell boy" hurt more than anything. Just going over the conversation again in his head sent his belly grinding. How come no matter what direction I go in in this city, I'm hitting my head on every hard object in sight? It all gave him gas.

He rummaged around in the legal folder he used as his portable desk drawer. Where are those stamps? Got to mail this letter. I didn't use them all. He dumps the whole folder on the floor. Envelopes. Loose leaf paper. Pencils. Pens. A ruler. Paper clips. A small spiral notebook labeled "Acting." He lifts each item again and again as if this might make the stamps, just one stamp, magically appear. He knew Aunt Myrt had two stamps left in her kitchen drawer. No, I can't do that. Aunt Myrt needs those stamps for the rent, the electric.

He had enough money to take the subway to work and back for tomorrow, Wednesday, and then Thursday he'd finally get paid. The hotel only pays every two weeks and tips well, tips. The singer's beautiful face gone ugly stormed back into his head. So I'm needing fare for Thursday too cause I can't get to the check cashing place till Friday. And that's if I don't buy food. Maybe Aunt Myrt decides she wants to cook something maybe for me without me asking or after I take someone's bags to a room at the hotel there might be a room service cart in the hallway waiting for a busboy and maybe I can swipe something off it. Like a beggar mouse. Me, begging.

Concentrate, Chet. No tears. Food. If I don't buy food. Let me count what I got after the subway. He started to count and stopped. What did it matter? I'm sitting here and crazy cause I don't have enough money to buy a stamp for Teenie's letter. To buy anything. You can't buy stamps and you think you're gonna buy Teenie some fancy wheelchair? You're the biggest fool since Goofy.

heart in my throat

Imagine. Me. In a car service cab in the middle of the night. A black car. A limo. Well, almost. Like some rich girl picking up the phone and saying I'm here and come pick me up at such and such time. It's got these maroon leather seats and a perfumey crown hanging off the driver's rear view mirror. Imagine me.

I couldn't let him come to the apartment. Not with Mother. She's there, not there, everywhere. Still. Forever? No, it's still Mother's place and I would feel her eyes. Right now is right now. And I'm in a car. And the truth is, I've got the money too. I mean, be realistic Pammy. Didn't Mother always plow it into me? "When I go, you still get the Social. You go right down there and tell them you still get it. Promise me." Well, I will and it won't have to stretch like Saran Wrap over the two of us. It'll be extra for me. I've got my office salary and now I'll have extra.

It was a totally new thought for her. Everything in those moments was totally new for her. Across the seat, the other window was slightly open from a previous passenger. She didn't want to lean over to close it and risk the chance of looking peculiar to the driver. And she also didn't want to ask if there was some way he could shut it from the panel of buttons beside him. Somewhere in the back of her brain schooled in Mrs. Margaret P. Kemple etiquette was that you didn't have a conversation with the driver if you were brought up rich. Thank you, Mother. Then I'll just enjoy the wind. Enjoy. Another totally novel thought. And the night coolness ran across her left ear and grazed her cheek. She felt like she was outside the car, running forward. She was the hood ornament slicing life, all the negative alternatives behind her.

Miss? That'll be thirty dollars. He thought he saw a look of terror on her face. Maybe she doesn't have the dough. Maybe she's gonna stiff me. But Pammy rooted around in her purse and pulled out two twenties.

Thank you. Keep the change.

adding the twos and the twos

He shut the door behind her. She stood stock still and looked around the studio. The futon on the floor. The pile of books and cd's. The boom box lying on its side.

Here. Let me take your coat.

The little corner kitchen looked sad to her. The tiniest four-burner stove she had ever seen with a little half-refrigerator next to it. On top of the fridge was a make-shift kitchen counter and atop of that—atop of that—

The industrial sized jar of French's Yellow Mustard gave her the best of shivers. She turned around and looked hard and softly at George.

You must really like mustard.
I like French's Mustard.

Then she knew what they really had in common. The ingenuity of obsession, the stalker gene. Pammy realized how deep their love could go and that she'd never have to stand in the cold street aching for a glimpse of George. He was here with her. He'd be here with her for as long as forever.

George grinned at Pammy.

I dusted the place after you called.

recruitment line

I am lying here next to her and she is totally ignorant. He pushed his hips closer against Valerie's sleeping buttocks not out of desire but as a seeker of warmth in the chilly loft. I feel unstoppable. I am unstoppable. I am a producer. My construct is taking shape.

Am I not always giving my students that claptrap about the bold move? When was the last time I took a bold move? Marrying Valerie? Well, now I free myself of her. Deliciously bold move, Mister Blessing.

The date was set. The cast must be assembled and yes, he had succeeded on that front as well. Succeed. Success. Calvert, success and you and New Jersey, happy together.

He had called Chet first. He was handsome and black. Cal knew he was swoon material and would be a great hit. But the child is so unsure of himself. I will have to build him up. Assure him that he is capable of many things. And one of them is earning large sums of money.

Was it timing? He had doubted he could corral him into the scheme for a measly fifteen hundred dollars and was surprised when Chet said yes. Cal thought even Chet seemed surprised after he had said it. But he had said the yes and Cal was determined to hold him to that agreement.

We have all done things, Chet. If I felt comfortable naming names, big names, I would but discretion is important among those of us in the thespian clan. I believe you are one of us or I never would have broached the subject. Ours is a profession of lean times dominating, so we must fend and survive accordingly. Welcome. Let this be your rite of passage.

The hook was in his tongue and barely a wriggle. Got him.

Wissa required a different approach. He had felt a certain savviness about her tempered by the wariness of sadness. Truly, I am a student of human nature. Look how many humans have passed through these loft doors alone. Do I not amuse myself with each and every one of them? I know what to do. I am skilled in what to do.

He assured Wissa she would not be alone performing for strangers. She would have Chet. She would have me. I am your teacher. The word teacher was her cue to confess her hunger to learn, to go to some world class conservatory. With tears no less. Surely all the planets must be aligned for her to spew so willingly. She is actually following the same script as I am. Halleluyah, I am a born again liar. Let me be your facilitator, sweet Wissa. Let me add to your educational fund. You shall be educated in no time at all.

Calvert felt Valerie shudder an arrhythmic breath beside him. I am unstoppable. I have paid my ticket to ride.

a bitter digestivo

Cold down in the subway. Dark cutting cold of the night. Anton was big in the chest glowing from the day. I have my line. I say my line one time. Two time and the director say we got it. And everyone is hurry off the set and on to somewhere I don't know. The assistant director he makes me sign the papers. Thank you very much Mr. Grybowski. A pleasure working with you. A pleasure working with me.

Anton didn't want to go home. He wanted to stay in the land of make believe forever. I will have a credit with my name. They check the spelling many times. It will say: Thug — Anton Grybowski. Me. Me. Me. Anton didn't want to tuck his happiness back into the basement shadows. He heard the subway in the distance. I want to roar. I want to make a big noise.

He looked to his left toward the sound of the approaching train. His eyes met a pair of angry eyes tucked below a heavy brow. Lipsticked lips anchored a snarl.

What you want?
I look for the train.

No. You look at me, asswipe. I seen ya.

Angry Eyes strode into Anton's face.

I don't like ya lookin' at me.
I look for the train. I look for the light. This is all.
And you talk funny. Hurt my ears. Just shut up. Shut up and go home bad man.

And with that, she gave Anton a quick shove and sent him falling onto the tracks. The uptown C train conductor was too close to stop. There was no music to the brakes. No music at all. No closing credits. A cacophony of screech and scream and simple, endless quiet. The acting universe was back in order.

light already through the blinds

Pammy saw stains on the sheets. He probably never even washes them. There was something rank about the whole room but it felt warm and comfortable to her. She liked the heft of him, the fuzziness of him beside her. George's eyes were open.

What was it like?
Huh?
What was it like? What does it feel like to be inside me?
Tight.
Hurtful tight?
Did I hurt you, Pammy?
No. Well, a little. But not really. No.
Well, you didn't hurt me neither.
Just asking.

George raised himself on his elbow. She was so small. She was his. She genuinely wanted to know his opinion. My opinion matters. My words matter. Think George, think. Rise up.

But what was it like? I'm just curious. To be inside me, you know.

What is she asking? How can I answer? I never thought those words. I'm usually thinking about me. Yeah, George, about you. I'm glad it's not really a monster cock. Never want to hurt her. Not her. But in my brain.

He looked at Pammy and, for the first time, saw freckles all across her shoulders and that her nipples were closest as anything to red and hard even now. He had never seen anyone, anyone so delicious. He knew the words, the answer to give her. His Pammy.

Inside. Inside you felt like a— like a warm papaya.

He felt elevated and poetic. A chivalrous knight. He turned and tucked his arms around her in a perfect spoon of warmth and trust. She nestled her rear into his hairy belly, the tickling tip of his penis. The feel of his balls. Every part of her as honest and open and naive as always.

What's a papaya?

the sun in my room

He sat on the futon gazing at his one teal wall. It was the right color for the right day. Teal, that cross between the blue of day and the blue of night. The phone will ring within the next half hour. Seamus clutched his red pillow to his belly. The phone will ring in the next half hour. Because manners tell you never to call before nine in the morning but if you just can't wait and you're just holding your breath, you call around 9:20 just to appear slightly casual.

And he would do that. He will call me. He won't leave me hanging. Not him. I know that already. This is dating, Seamus. This is hello how are you who are you even before a chest hair is exposed. I hope he has dark hair on his chest. I don't care what he has on his chest.

That night when he went to Bibi's, he felt he had been caught in an avalanche. The boulders of hurt that sobbed and thundered from her. He never held anyone so tightly. Every Bibi word slapped his heart, made him want to find her family and kill them. You were just a baby. A little girl. How could they?

He offered to stay the night but she sent him home. On the train, he sat, every part of him feeling more and more hollow. The osmosis of grief and pain had left him in pieces. Seamus couldn't leave the subway. He kept changing trains. Downtown. Uptown. He stared at the white tiles in almost empty stations until the next train arrived.

He found himself on the uptown C train and without thinking got off at 72nd Street. He climbed the stairs and into the wind on Central Park West. Seamus glanced up at the silhouette of the Dakota against the clouds and gave his respects to John Lennon and "Rosemary's Baby" and crossed the street into the park. It's a warm night for winter and no snow for a while. Someone will be there.

His feet progressed to the Ramble, home to birds and anonymous nocturnal entanglements. It's not courage that's bringing me here. And it has nothing to do with want. All those times I chickened out. Couldn't leave the pavement. Hesitation in the face of vegetation. Yeah, right, Seamus. Fear. But tonight I want the threat, the salt of violence. The possibility my face will be punched into that cum condom fertilized dirt. If I can take one quarter of what poor Bibi —

The dark of night was darker under the canopy of branches in The Ramble. Quiet. Stillness. The paths too twisty for the hiss of wind to intrude. The crack of a twig felt like an eruption. Seamus froze.

Would he be in leather? Spikes and piercings? Muscles impervious to the cold? An angry curve to his lip? Would he say nothing?

Just unzip and shove me down on the boot packed ground.

Seamus heard footsteps closing in on him. He was face to face with eyes larger than the glasses struggling to surround them. A mouth as agape as Seamus's.

Umm, I have a big banana.

Seamus pivoted and ran up the path and out of the park. Giggles propelled him. He caught his breath at the avenue. Banana Boy was suddenly beside him.

I'm sorry.
That was the worst line ever. Ever.
My first time. I'm sorry. Thought it would sound tough.

Banana Boy dug deep into his pea coat pocket, pulled out a wrinkled black yarmulke and clipped it onto his hair.

You've got to be kidding. You took off your yarmulke to go to The Ramble?
It didn't seem Kosher.

The giggles came back. Banana Boy caught the contagion. The laughter felt good and easy. Seamus paid closer attention. He looked into the awkward deep set eyes behind the glasses and knew. Seamus knew.

Coffee?

please help me i'm falling

Wissa dialed Chet.

He didn't tell us how to dress. How to dress for the party. You know. Is it dressy or casual?
This is my aunt's phone. I shouldn't even of answered.
But how do we dress? It's tomorrow.
We're getting undressed. I'm not renting a tux.
I'm serious. Call him, Chet. You call him, please. It's almost time. Less than twenty-four hours.
No. They're gonna have cocktails and stuff. You call him. Use the emergency cell he gave us if it's such an emergency. I gotta go.

She stared at the phone. Chet didn't sound scared. He sounded angry. I don't like men. I don't like him. I don't like Cal. I'm making a mistake but I said yes. Wissa, it'll only be like an hour and you never have to think again on any of this and Cal promised two thousand and that can cover my first year of school, I think. I should've looked it up before I said yes but I think that's enough. Certainly not going to look it up now and be disappointed. What if I'm wrong and it's not enough and I've gone and done this? This.

One thing at a time. I've got to know what to wear. She called Cal. Cal was curt.

It is a dinner party in a ten room apartment on Central Park West. Dress appropriately. You have watched a sufficient amount of television, I imagine. And, please, bathe.

And with that, he hung up on her.
Bathe? That's what he thinks of me. What am I doing? What am I doing?

consequences of the positive

Bibi decided to go to work early. Very early. Nobody works the trains for spare change that early. Especially her. Especially Mami. The Mami subway invasion still rattled her. She could take me with her. She could take me down to the never again. No. I be in the subway by six, absolute latest. And I ain't gonna be body squeezed in no rush hour train no more. Not never. I'll be like those rich people in their limos. They don't want us touching them. Us peons. Another favorite GED diploma word. They don't want to touch us neither. Especially in the summer and some girl's long frizzy hair gets caught in your armpit. Or winter and some skanky bed bug guy in an old raggy jacket gotta spread his contagious just by being pushed close. No. Not me after today. From now on I'll make my own limo subway. So early, it'll be me and all the empty seats. And most times, I never get to sit down but now I will. Spread out and everything. Relax. Smart idea, Bibi.

But when she got on the train around 5:45 a.m., every seat was already taken. Not the no exhaling allowed like at rush hour, but full nevertheless. I guess these are all the guys behind the griddle making the egg sandwiches, the regular coffees. And look.

All of them asleep. Guess this is a pretty safe place to sleep in the morning. No Mami's hoping to get nickels and dimes off this hungry crowd.

Some of the lights were still off in the lobby of her office building and it seemed strange not seeing Jimmy the security guard. She nodded to the night guard half asleep on a stool. I'll know your name soon enough. And maybe I'll let you know mine.

The elevator door opens on the eighth floor to the law firm where she spends her paralegal days. There's a guy waiting for the elevator. A guy hoping to sneak out for a little fresh air to wake himself up for the rest of his shift. A guy around thirty with dreams of making a name via the world of words in his head. A guy who works the lobster shift as a proofreader to make those dreams erupt.

The elevator door opens on the eighth floor and Bibi is startled to find herself almost face to face with someone about to get in. It's the guy. He takes one look at her. One look electric. The surprise of her tumble of black hair. The intensity of her eyes.

There's no way you're on the lobster shift too. You look like dawn.

Bibi can't help but smile at his compliment. They're both just standing there. Standing. And his hand reaches out to keep the elevator door open.

I've never seen you in proofreading. And never on this floor. Wait, it's coming to me. I know why we've never met. We must be in parallel worlds.

You're going break the elevator.
Oh, it's not going anywhere.
Yeah, well you're making sure of that.
I believe having the elevator here is somehow keeping you here.
You're keeping me here.

It just escaped her. Where did that come from? You're keeping me here.

A playful flirt. Flirting. She'd seen it in movies, on tv, but out of her mouth? Even now, right in this very moment, his face made no clear impression. If she turned around she probably wouldn't be able to describe him. But his voice. It purred inside her.

Hey, where did you go? Your thoughts went somewhere else, didn't they Mystery Girl?
My thoughts?
Your thoughts. Your everything. Don't disappear on me. Besides, you now know where to find me. Proofreading. Eighth floor. Lobster shift. But you, you could be the delusion of too much caffeine or a bit of Ebenezer Scrooge's undigested beef.

He sees that the Dickens reference is totally lost upon her. He extends his hand for a shake.

How do you do? I'm Adam. And I'd very much like to meet you.

the possibilities

All afternoon he had thought of contacting another one of Valerie's clients. I should have a certain momentum going. What does it matter that this debut performance has not even occurred? It is all at hand. It will all go forward. Perhaps I should wait, though.

Cal had not noticed that Valerie's second rolodex of business contacts was no longer available to him. No longer sitting like a golden Ferris wheel on her desk. Well, he had noticed it but assumed that in one of her periodic cleaning bouts she had taken it off the desk and tucked it into a drawer. Hubris had set him free from any hint of paranoia. I did it. By the end of this evening, my hand will hold ten thousand dollars in cash from Schuyler Titus. Horny Schuyler Titus. Thirty-five hundred for the kids and the rest for me.

Well, this is my practice financial run. In the future, the money shall increase. There are risks. There must be compensation. I shall become a better businessman. My twenty percent will always be on the top. Why stop at twenty? I could go for twenty-five. Most important, I will deal only with high end customers. Class.

Who is to know that this is the first time I have orchestrated such an event? I am an actor. I excel at lies. As long as everyone is satisfied in the truest sense of the word.

What are you getting dressed up for?
One of my students, Valerie dear. I promised him I would attend a one-act he is in. One of those horrid drafty black box theaters. If I were smart, I would be sporting long johns.
But the sapphire cuff links?
I prefer to look my best at all times. You know that.

Valerie went back to her business magazine. God, he's so full of shit. He could really be doing this. Am I just being way too suspicious? I should wait to hear from that detective. But look at him. Where is he going? Calm down. He'll be followed. He'll be followed. It's worth every dollar.

Cal checked his watch. They are probably sitting down to dinner now. I am not being treated with respect. I had thought he would ask me to dine as well. No. Schuyler instructed — instructed — me to arrive after dinner. Well, perhaps in time for a glass of port. If he feels generous. I am providing the after dinner entertainment. I have morphed into a Barnum for the elite. Remember your goals, Calvert. Remember everything.

pep talk

I can do this. I can man up. Wissa will keep me calm. She has focus. Hey, she didn't have much focus on the phone yesterday. She was wigging out. I was the calm one. Well, maybe she gets rid of all her stuff before and we walk in there like some peaceful Hari Krishna.

Do I think about her? About Wissa? I haven't ever thought about her before. Not like that. Not enough to get hard. I mean she's kind of scrawny and I'm not that much into white. How do I not look at all the people? How many people will there be? Cal mentioned maybe tips. Will I get so much money I have to do major taxes? I mean on top of the fifteen hundred he's promising maybe they'll slip me another thousand. Wait, did he really even mention tips or was it me in my head? But if so, tips— that's a serious adjustment against last year's AGI. Stop. If I think about taxes, I probably won't get hard. Asshole. You're not playing bookkeeper here. This isn't side work sorting some guy's W2's and a shoebox full of receipts. This is cash. This is invisible. The tax man don't know nothing about sex. Chet stopped thinking entirely for a moment.

And neither do I.

I have to stop thinking. But I have to think of somebody to think of to get hard. Someone I can shut my eyes and be in my own head like I'm about to sleep or just wake up. Oh, I know who. I'll think about Nessy Marie, that girl in math class who disappeared. She was so pretty and shy. Somehow she got gobbled up. No one ever knew where. She smiled at me every day. And I never said hello back. That was the trigonometry class. That was the year I was trying to be tough and where did it get me? Biceps and his gang still called me a down-low-no-go and I never spoke with Nessy Marie or smelled her or felt her softness. And now she's gone. Probably in some swamp. And here I am in the swamp of New York. Something swampy about Cal for sure. But it's money. And if I'm going to stay, it's money. And if I'm going to be any help to Teenie, it's money. It's money. It's money. Ah, Nessy Marie, I'll think of your smooth molasses skin and I'll get hard.

résumé on my body

She had planned on taking a quick disco nap after work but her adrenalin production was in overdrive. Instead, she put some witch hazel on cotton balls and rested them on her eyelids. Relax. Relax. Up she jumped from the bed. Relaxation was futile. She showered hot hot water until her hand was almost too slow to turn it down. Lotion everwhere. She took extra care with her makeup. Waterproof. Use everything waterproof. She got a q-tip and cleaned the lint from her belly button. Do you really think that's where they'll be looking, Wissa?

She knew now the money wouldn't be enough for even a semester. But this could be a serious down payment and probably show some bank I'm a good saver from the job at Dolan's and that I'm a really prime candidate to give a student loan to. And then I'll be set. Go to real classes all day long. With people who really want to be actors and teachers who don't run side shows.

I'm the side show. Is this the crazy reckless me actually coming out again? After Victor, it was anyone. It just felt good. So good the feel of flesh. Stop. If I keep going in these circles. She reached for the bottle of deep blue tablets in the medicine cabinet. Preventive medicine. Thank you God, that I'm okay today. I'll take an extra one just to be sure. But at this moment and for tonight, my body is clean. But all this worrying. It's always big emotion that brings it on. Maybe if I take two, it'll head it off at the pass. But tonight – I feel nothing. None of the warning signs. None of the tingling. The pain out of proportion. She listened to her body intently. No. Nothing. Tomorrow, though, I'll probably have it.

Chet is so okay. I'm so glad it's him and not some stranger and not anyone else in the class. Chet is sweet. I would never. Not to him. Not to anyone. The most hateful person I ever met — I would never put them at risk. My worst enemy. Do I have any enemies? That's not the point. I'll pay for this tomorrow but please, please God, keep my body clean for tonight. No herpes outbreaks, please. The jokes. The dread. Truth? Most everybody has it. This I know. Only the girl scouts announce. Or the fools. Or me. Careful little Wissa swaddled in her undies on days not fit to share. Let me blow you instead. Your turn to be happy.

When is it my turn? Who the hell was the bastard gave it to me anyhow?

anticipation

While the doorman made his required announcement call, Cal absorbed the lobby. The subtle dark wallpaper. The Oriental rugs. He recognized a Hamedan. The early twentieth century reproductions of Louis XV chairs, Rococo in the extreme. Cal knew antiques. That head crammed with useless knowledge never used. Until now. I will talk to Schuyler about these antiques. We can discuss my long-held observation that the lobbies of many New York buildings, in all boroughs, have never undergone any redecoration since they were erected. Consequently, they hold a trove of antiques, some, I imagine, of great value. Schuyler will be impressed.

Sir? Sir? Mr. Blessing?
Yes.
Mr. Titus says you are to go up.

Cal stepped towards the elevators.

No, not that way. Service is over there.
You are not serious. The service elevator?
Mr. Titus said.

a short walk on central park west

Chet arrived at 96th Street first. He wished Wissa had gotten there before him. What if she chickens out? How long do I stand on this corner? Do I still go? Will I have to fuck some strange old lady or something? Come on, Wissa. Get here.

She tapped him on the shoulder and he instinctively jumped. Heart thumping.

I'm glad it's you. I didn't tell you that.
I'm glad it's you, too.

He was lying but who would he have been glad to be doing this with? No one. I want to get the hell out of here. Now.

They walked uptown. One doorman building. Two. People passed them. Solos walking dogs. Couples dressed up to go out. As they got closer to the this-is-it building, Wissa touched Chet's forearm to stop him.

I have to be honest about something. Please don't freak out. Because I would never put you in an unsafe place. I mean, it's actually only catching when you're having an outbreak.

Outbreak? What are you talking about?

I have herpes.

Whoa—

Wait, Chet, this is the way it works. Honest. I always know before I'm even going to have an outbreak 'cause your nerves are involved and you, I, really feel this warning. And you can actually only get it if someone's having an outbreak and you actually touch it like right on the outbreak and that's not going to happen.

But I'm hearing herpes is always contagious. Always there.

That's what the drug people say. They want to sell pills. If you speak to a doctor. My doctor. Three quarters of the country has herpes and you just live with it. But the pills keep the outbreaks down.

But how do you know for sure when it's inside you and all? Maybe your nerves don't always tell you.

Okay Chet. I didn't mean for this to become a class.

She hated this. She hated this. How many times had she given this same speech? I need a blackboard and chalk. Diagrams. A white lab coat. Oh, God help me, I will have to make this speech for the rest of my life.

Chet, I told you, I feel it. Big time warning. 'Cause it's nerve endings. And it's not inside. Not for me. Listen, if you had herpes on your ass and I put my thigh there, then I would forever get my outbreaks where my thigh touched you. Get it? So, for a fact, I don't have it inside. It's where some guy's balls hit me.

Chet cringed.

And I don't get outbreaks that often and don't have it today or now. Absolutely nothing. And, I said, I'd never put you in danger. I've never put anyone in danger or even accidentally passed it on.
Then why'd you bother telling me?
I have to be honest. Especially tonight. It would kill me if I wasn't.

He farted.

Fuck, Wissa, you had to add to my gas? What if I fart up there? What if I get the fucking runs?
You won't. You're on stage. We're acting.

She took his hand and they continued walking.

merchant chafing

The cook opened the door and told him to take a seat at the kitchen table.

Mr. Titus will be with you soon.

I cannot believe this indignity. I am sitting at a table piled high with dirty dishes. Dishes by all rights I should have been dining from. This is outrageous. I am absolutely amazed by his effrontery. It is my wife who put the food on those plates. My wife who advised Schuyler Titus regarding investments that netted him this penthouse. My wife.

My wife who caused me to create this plan in the first place. Have I made a mistake? No. I am using my wits to gain my freedom. This is, as they say, a slight hiccup. He is treating me as if I were a procurer which I am definitely not. I am an artist. An impresario and this is my art.

Cal.

Schuyler Titus greeted him warmly. Shook Calvert's hand vigorously.

I hope Hortensia here offered you some dessert. It was magnificent. Bananas Foster.
None left, sir.
Oh, no worries. We'll fix Cal up with a glass of port when I bring him inside.

Schuyler sat down with Cal at the kitchen table and lowered his voice. His conspiratorial voice took over. Rumbly. Almost seductive. He pulled a thick envelope from his breast pocket and handed it to Cal.

There we go, Cal.

Calvert glanced at the cook. He is doing this in front of his cook. And now a server is coming back in with more dishes. Is this a public event? Schuyler followed his eye line.

Oh, don't worry about them. We're practically family. Don't ask, don't tell, don't peek. Money brings you discretion, old boy.

I am not your boy. I am G. Calvert Blessing. But the envelope felt good in his hand and he flash imagined counting all the dollars and felt a slight tingle in his penis at the thought. And that slight tingle put a lock on his mouth.

I'm assuming they'll be prompt. Shall we be going in now? By the way, Cal, my wife thought it would be a nice, albeit decadent, touch if they were on the floor.
On the floor?
Well, not entirely. She has an old mink coat that was in the give-away pile. She thought it would be a nice touch if they were lying on it. Creative, don't you think, Cal?

Calvert followed Schuyler into the living room. I wish he would cease calling me Cal. It sounds disrespectful coming out of his mouth. An excess of buddy, buddy. I believe I am having a frisson of regret.

The chatter in the room evaporated into silence when Calvert entered. My god, they are all staring at me. Staring.

Friends, this is our master of ceremonies, Cal Blessing.
Calvert.
Yes, Calvert it is. Actually, though, we really don't need to know anyone's names now do we? First or last. So I will hold off on the introductions. Those of us who know— know.

The guests inhaled that whiff of exclusivity. Cal bristled. Well, now they know my name, thank you very much. "Master of ceremonies." Please save me. Be calm, Calvert. Minor indignities. All minor.

The house buzzer rang and Schuyler went to answer it. Cal could hear his reply all too clearly.

Send them up. The front elevator.

Schuyler's wife Dolly winked at Cal. She reached over to the couch and grabbed a lush mink coat. She waved it like a toreador to a bull.

Olé! Olé!

Everyone in the room laughed the anxious, high-pitched laugh of giddy children one foot onto a roller coaster. Cal's forced smile was more of a constipated grimace.

up up and

The doorman directed them up to the penthouse. Wissa's hands were cold. Her Reynaud's Syndrome was acting up and the middle finger on her right hand was gone. Ice white. Numb. No circulation whatsoever. She rubbed it to try and get the blood flowing. Bad time to lose my circulation.

She looked over at Chet. Head tilted upward. He was totally focused on the floor numbers progressing to the penthouse. She saw something white by his sideburn and realized it was shaving cream foam. She flicked it off.

What was that for?
Something on you.

His face was tight.

I really do have gas something awful.
Better now than later. Go for it.

He let out a series of bullet thumps. They laughed. They both felt better.

Chet, oh man, serious gas. That smelled like frankfurters. Were you eating frankfurters? Totally inappropriate.
Totally.

Now they were a team. Wissa gave his hand a quick squeeze.

am i are we

Am I in my body? Are we lying here on this floor? Are there people around us? I can no longer see, remember their faces. I don't want to remember their faces. I blot them out. My eyes are closed. All I feel is Chet and he's hurting me. I'm so dry and he's pounding. I should make noise. He's making none. Nothing at all. I should make noise. Act, Wissa, act.

A man's voice chimed in from the left.
Fuck her. Fuck her hard.

When they came into the room, Cal took them briefly aside to whisper whisper whisper. The most potent aphrodisiacs are power, humor and money. Tonight, in this room, two out of three. Remember you are the sexiest people in the room. They are all watching you. You are the stars. They want to be you. They want to be you being fucked. Words both Chet and Wissa had heard in class. Class. So distant. So irrelevant.

Chet made a little eeeeee sound and his body jerked. He came. I should come too. I'll arch my back. I'll push my hips hard against him. I'll pretend I'm not so raw that I expect to see blood when I open my eyes.

They stopped moving.

Schuyler looked at his wife Dolly who smiled at the Heinzes, Lester and Estelle. They shared a glance with Harvey and Mariella, Cousin Ott and Kitty. What a fun evening. They were all hot. They wanted more. Schuyler understood. He wanted more as well.

Say, Cal, how about a little one on one? Remuneration is a given.

Dolly's mouth was close to Schuyler's ear.

How about your young man here takes a little walk with my sweet wife to the master bedroom? I believe he has the stamina. And this lovely with the beautiful mouth might, perhaps, come with me to my study?

Schuyler's erection was evident to all.

After that — my friends here. Your kids are young. Energetic. What do you say, Cal?

Cal looked at Wissa and Chet. They were all trapped. They were all wanting to run. In unison, they made a slow nod to each other.

And they stayed.

no glow

The cold air was better than any shower. Cal had left with them and at the next corner they stopped and he distributed the cash. I don't care if Cal makes a mistake. Just let it be a mistake in my favor.

I do not care if I make a mistake. The children, in truth, deserve all this money. Stop yourself right there, Calvert. You made this happen. You do care. Count quickly and efficiently. Quickly. I cannot look at them.

Very good, Chet and Wissa. We shall regroup and perhaps —

One glance told him they would never sign on again. Cal hailed a cab.

Wissa remembered that speed blink moment looking up from the mink and seeing Calvert touching himself. She held tighter onto Chet's hand.

Please. I don't want to be alone tonight.

He snuggled his head into her hair. He had never felt so close to another human being, not Teenie, no one. A tear from his cheek fell onto hers.

Stay with me. Stay with me.

They hugged deeply, reverently. Central Park West would never be under their feet again.

the wake up

It was the first warm day. One of those freak warm days in March that fools you into believing the sun has true warmth, such warmth that you can shed your layers bare your legs risk a tan. The first warm day. People felt released from winter. Emboldened. Giddy with a cloudless sky.

Maura walked up the avenue. Errands. A destination. But what did it matter? She thought of 18th Street and all those people. If I were to go back there it would be an empty space. A fly by night. A night that flew by and what did it leave?

I am just Maura. Not defined by Gus. Not defined by my friendship with Nan. She thought of all the men who had been inside her in the last years. How empty that all felt. And that class. That last bit of homework. Even that. That class was a ruse. Dollars for some fantasy of a class. Were each one of us in our own sexual fantasy and Calvert our group leader to nowhere? How weird. I'm not sure I want to credit that guy with even that much intelligence. But still. Some kind of racket and he did get money out of each and every one of us. I'm sure there will a whole room full of sexual hopefuls for his next semester. And all of them thinking that that class has meaning.

The sun felt so good that she didn't even want to walk. Walking creates a breeze. If I stand right here I can absorb all that warmth like a lizard on a rock.

Up ahead, she heard some music. Why does music sound so much more alive out of doors? Maura set her feet to walking again. Across the street, a stooped, gray-haired black man was playing a trumpet. Playing Fats Waller's "Jitterbug Waltz" and the music put its arms around Maura and made her body want to spin. She crossed the street to get closer. She carefully placed a dollar in his trumpet case. If the wind blew all his dollars away, would people give them back? For this music, I would run all over the neighborhood to retrieve his dollars.

Thank you, ma'am.
No, the thanks go to you for making this an even more beautiful day.

Even the "ma'am" didn't cold water her day. Something had changed. Something was changing. And all this time, she thought she had been standing still.

chewing on the inside of my brain

Valerie did something she hadn't done in years, not since she lost the Freeborn family account on her thirtieth birthday and thought her career was over. Well, it wasn't and here she was full circle. Full circle? Not quite. A different kettle of fish altogether, Aunt Mush would say. She shut the door of her office. She told her assistant Caitlyn to hold all her calls. Then she rummaged around in the bottom drawer of her desk until she found the box of chocolates. The cheap box of chocolates probably bought last minute at the drug store. The cheap box of chocolates delivered by messenger two Christmases ago from the little stationery store around the corner so desperate to keep from going under, anxious to keep her company's account. Well, they were gone and here she was rooting around the desperation box. Two years ago, she had made a big show of throwing out the candy and then secretly retrieved it from the garbage. In the back of her mind, even then, she knew the chocolates should be kept in case of emergency.

In case of emergency. She opened the brown envelope again. These pictures. How did he even get them? He had mentioned the house staff. But how? Oh, me. Yes you, Valerie. You passed on the information about Cal conferring with Schuyler Titus at the gala. You were the one speculating that Titus could have said yes when you were hoping, hoping he had said no. Hoping Titus had half the moral backbone of whistle blower Monroe Cabell. Look at these photos, oh God. There isn't a vertebra in the room. Well, it was my heads up that probably gave the detective time to make the connections, grease the palms that cooked or cleaned in Schuyler's building. Schuyler Titus. Such a good client. Well, you don't have to lose him. Not really. Just Cal.

The chocolates had a whitish tinge to them. They tasted like cardboard. One after the other, she crammed them into her mouth.

He bribed the staff. That's what the detective must have done. He bribed the staff to take these disgusting photos. Most of the faces didn't look familiar. But there's Cal in the background, totally in focus. And he doesn't look altogether happy. Good. He's going to be a lot less happy.

Am I doing something that can't be undone? If I make a phone call am I pulling the switch on my own electric chair? But what has he done for me? And even now, I'm not really sure what he's been up to but it doesn't smell right. Get real. Look at those pictures. He did that. He made that happen. Those kids certainly don't know Schuyler Titus. I wonder how much money changed hands? I wonder what he's planning to do with it? What he's planning to do next?

Oh Cal, don't do this to me. Don't do anything to me. Why can't we just keep going in the non-direction we've been going in for years? If this private detective has found something, do I have to act? I don't think the detective can blow a whistle if I don't. Isn't that professional discretion or something? I'm the one who's in control. I'm the paying client.

I like my life. I like what I have. What do I have? I have money, respect, a warm body in my bed. Calvert. Mommy called you a self-absorbed pompous popinjay not two days before she and Daddy died. What would she say now? A panderer. She would probably say we should have had a pre-nup. Well, no one had pre-nups back then.

You are cruel. You are cruel to me. And for no reason at all. All these years I could have been in an apartment with a doorman and a real elevator that works instead of our make-believe artsy fartsy loft. Yes, I could have been a pretender. And I was.

I'm truly scared. Me.

The chocolates were gone. She wished there were more. She put the empty box back in her desk drawer. She checked her teeth in a mini magnifying mirror from her purse. Back to work, Valerie. It's what you do best.

john donne, ann donne, undone

Mr. Blessing?
Who is there?
I'm Detective Lazarowitz, New York City Police Department. Tenth Precinct.
How do I know that to be true?
If you come downstairs, sir, I'll show you identification.

Cal took his finger off the intercom. Am I going downstairs? Am I going to hell? To jail? What do they know? Who would even have told them? Certainly all involved have something to lose, especially the children. Perhaps the landlord sent the police. Our illegal renovations. After all these years? You wish it were the landlord. No. Do not close your eyes, Calvert. You know. And somehow the police know as well.

I shall make the pre-emptive strike. I have learned this from every police procedural television show that Valerie watches so religiously and every low brow crime film she has insisted we view. Film noir, my arse. I shall call my attorney. Yes.

The buzzer rang again. Cal flung open all the drawers to

Valerie's little desk. What happened to that goddamned rolodex? He pulled a manila folder from the file cabinet nearby. Searched legal papers for a phone number and dialed.

David? This is Calvert Blessing.
Yes?
David, I believe I may require your services.
Apologies, Calvert, but I am Valerie's attorney, not yours.
What? But you have done our wills, our—
Do you need me to recommend a criminal attorney?
A criminal attorney?

The buzzer. The buzzer. Why would David even suspect I would require a criminal attorney? Stop that buzzing already. I cannot breathe.

I cannot breathe.

ring ring

He had a friend who clerked downtown. Clerked at the district attorney's office. It was simple bar gossip to fill the air at The Sweet William. Seamus was there as a couple. At last I'm a couple. And his friend the clerk so happy to see Seamus at last with a beau at his side was chattering on when suddenly Seamus's inner light bulb exploded. All the dots connected. Seamus couldn't dial the phone fast enough.

Ring. Ring.

Hey, Bibi, girl. It's Seamus. News flash. Oh, how the mighty have fallen. Don't think the insult king is holding that last class. Or any class ever again.

from here

Wissa and Chet walked out of the courthouse and onto Centre Street. Bad dream behind. They knew they were coated in luck or how else would the sun be shining upon them? No records to follow them. Every day a look ahead.

All this time, I never told Aunt Myrt. Explained it all by saying the hotel was short-handed and piling on the hours. Told her I was crashing with a friend who lived closer to the hotel. Yeah, like 73rd Street is really a hop skip from Hudson Street. Told the hotel my Aunt Myrt was ailing. Please, Jesus forgive me, don't make that story come true. Writing Teenie like the sun was still in the sky. And look here. It is.

Wissa gave his hand a squeeze. Who would have thought this shy, skinny guy would be my rock?

Move out of your aunt's.
Yeah. I've been thinking that too.

A hot dog stand was up ahead. Chet offered to treat. As they crossed the street, a woman sped by in a motorized wheel chair. First the hot dog, Chet thought.

the end rush to begin

Maura picked up the reddest fattest bunch of radishes. She felt a basket graze her side in the narrow grocery aisle. She turned to see the back of another gray hair. He was tall and lean. No love handles. No gut. Just the blessed gray hair of my tribe. Turn around. Turn around.

And he did.

He grinned at Maura. Her eyes answered him. Then she deliberately walked off to find out where they were hiding the Brussels sprouts. I will play hide and seek. And play is the operative word. How long has it been? Okay, let's see if you're searching for Brussels sprouts too, my friend. What fun. Everything about her smiled.

And across town Bibi lay on her bed, her newly installed ceiling fan lazily moving the blue sky spring air about. Adam had put it up for her. Adam the sweet surprise of her life. He sat in the corner, totally immersed in reading one of his beloved mysteries.

Bibi wrote a few lines in the drug store notebook on her lap.

Adam, he's always pushing me to write it down. Not so much push as gentle shove. Write it down. It's no way truly gone until you can stare at it on paper and say I been there and never go back. I have this life now. With Adam. He listened to the ugly and be wanting me still. Loves me. And Seamus, my wobbly searching friend. That makes a family. A new family. The old Bibi goes deep behind. Mami. Papi Fannon. I blast you. I blast you to nothing.

Bibi cupped her belly with her hand. Tomorrow I'll tell Adam. For now, it's my sweet secret joy, my life corrected.

K. Denmark has been a writer for many years — from advertising copywriter to non-fiction articles to screenplays. She is a published cartoonist and illustrator, plus a film and commercial sound technician with very observant ears. This is her first novel.

www.ingramcontent.com/pod-product-compliance
Lightning Source LLC
Chambersburg PA
CBHW020405260626
47156CB00007B/2239

* 9 7 9 8 2 1 8 1 5 8 7 5 0 *